"I'm doing a survey," Blake said. "I need to find out if you taste better than mint chocolate chip."

She was delicious, he decided an instant later. Nichelle moved closer to him as his lips met hers, caressing the nape of his neck with her fingers. He trailed his hand across the bare skin of her shoulders, igniting a heated path as he went. She arched against him, reveling in his strength.

"Don't wiggle," he commanded.

She wiggled. He moaned.

"You're not going to postpone discussing business by seducing me, Ms. Clay."

"Okay, okay, I'll get my tax forms," she said.

"What you're going to get," he said, lunging to his feet with her in his arms, "is me!" And then he carried her into the bedroom . . .

Bantam Books by Joan Elliott Pickart
Ask your bookseller for the titles you have missed.

BREAKING ALL THE RULES
(*Loveswept #61*)

CHARADE
(*Loveswept #74*)

THE FINISHING TOUCH
(*Loveswept #80*)

ALL THE TOMORROWS
(*Loveswept #85*)

LOOK FOR THE SEA GULLS
(*Loveswept #90*)

WAITING FOR PRINCE CHARMING
(*Loveswept #94*)

FASCINATION
(*Loveswept #99*)

THE SHADOWLESS DAY
(*Loveswept #105*)

SUNLIGHT'S PROMISE
(*Loveswept #110*)

RAINBOW'S ANGEL
(*Loveswept #114*)

MIDNIGHT RYDER
(*Loveswept #116*)

THE EAGLE CATCHER
(*Loveswept #138*)

JOURNEY'S END
(*Loveswept #146*)

MR. LONELYHEARTS
(*Loveswept #153*)

SECRETS OF AUTUMN
(*Loveswept #162*)

LISTEN FOR THE DRUMMER
(*Loveswept #166*)

KALEIDOSCOPE
(*Loveswept #179*)

WILD POPPIES
(*Loveswept #190*)

REFORMING FREDDY
(*Loveswept #204*)

WHAT ARE *LOVESWEPT* ROMANCES?

They are stories of true romance and touching emotion. We believe those two very important ingredients are constants in our highly sensual and very believable stories in the *LOVESWEPT* line. Our goal is to give you, the reader, stories of consistently high quality that may sometimes make you laugh, sometimes make you cry, but are always fresh and creative and contain many delightful surprises within their pages.

Most romance fans read an enormous number of books. Those they truly love, they keep. Others may be traded with friends and soon forgotten. We hope that each *LOVESWEPT* romance will be a treasure—a "keeper." We will always try to publish

LOVE STORIES YOU'LL NEVER FORGET
BY AUTHORS YOU'LL ALWAYS REMEMBER

The Editors

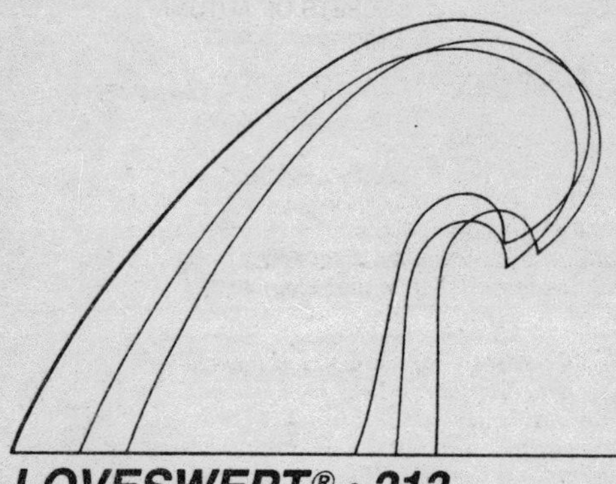

LOVESWEPT® • 213

Joan Elliott Pickart

Leprechaun

BANTAM BOOKS
TORONTO • NEW YORK • LONDON • SYDNEY • AUCKLAND

LEPRECHAUN
A Bantam Book / October 1987

If you would be interested in receiving protective vinyl covers for your Loveswept books, please write to this address for information:

Loveswept
Bantam Books
P.O. Box 985
Hicksville, NY 11802

ISBN 0-553-21838-7

Published simultaneously in the United States and Canada

Bantam Books are published by Bantam Books, Inc. Its trademark, consisting of the words "Bantam Books" and the portrayal of a rooster, is Registered in U.S. Patent and Trademark Office and in other countries. Marca Registrada. Bantam Books, Inc., 666 Fifth Avenue, New York, New York 10103.

PRINTED IN THE UNITED STATES OF AMERICA

O 0 9 8 7 6 5 4 3 2 1

For Alida Elizabeth Hunt
HAPPY BIRTHDAY!

One

The March wind whipping along the sidewalk reminded Nichelle of a frisky puppy engaged in undisciplined play with no regard for the consequences. Skirts were flipped upward, revealing women's legs, some shapely, some not so shapely. Newspapers were nudged from beneath men's arms, and expressive expletives followed after the wind.

Nichelle clamped her hand firmly on the crown of the floppy straw hat she wore, determined that it was going to stay in place. There was no way, *no way*, that she was entering the plush lobby of the Timberlane Towers apartment building with her green hair in plain view for all to see. In some anything-goes sections of Los Angeles the color of her hair wouldn't draw a flicker of attention. But Timberlane Towers? No way.

Never again, Nichelle thought, stomping along the sidewalk. Never again would she let Eric sweet-talk her into allowing him to practice his homework assignment on her. The fact that he was taking a beautician course by correspondence was absurd in the first place, especially since he had to scrounge up his own supplies. She'd told him to try the hot oil treatment on Kurt, but no-o-o Eric had said, it was a special concoction for blondes, and he desperately needed Nickie's hair.

"I'm going to kill him," she muttered now. It had been bad enough trying to sleep with a towel wrapped around her head all night. Then this morning—green hair that hadn't lightened one iota after three vigorous shampooings.

She'd stormed across the hall to pound on Eric's door only to be told by a groggy Kurt that Eric had left early to make deliveries for the grocery store.

"Look at my hair!" Nichelle had shrieked.

"Uh-oh," Kurt had said. "Not good. I guess you're a tad upset, huh?"

"No, not at all." She had smiled ever so sweetly. "Prepare to live off your memories of your time spent with your Eric because he's a dead man!"

"Now, Nickie, calm down. Eric will know what to do. He's brilliant."

"Love is so blind," she had said, rolling her eyes heavenward. "He's stupid. He's a menace."

"He's beautiful," Kurt had said dreamily.

"Oh, for Pete's sake," she had muttered, then flounced back to her apartment and slammed the door.

Now, here she was about to enter Timberlane Towers, wearing the dilapidated hat she'd found smushed in the back of her closet.

Oh, well, she thought, mentally shrugging. There

was nothing she could do about it now. She should be concentrating on today's fantasy of what Blake Tyrone Pemberton, Jr., looked like. Junior. That's what his mother had called him when she'd given Nichelle to him as a thirtieth birthday present three months ago.

Every Wednesday morning Nichelle traveled for an hour by bus to the edge of exclusive Bel Air, then walked the six blocks to Timberlane Towers. And every Wednesday morning she created a picture in her mind of what Junior looked like. She gathered the clues from her days spent in his apartment and, so far, had created some weird images of Mrs. Pemberton's baby boy.

Junior was tall, that much Nichelle knew for sure, due to the various jeans and slacks he left strewn around his bedroom. In one of her scenarios she'd pictured him as thin, balding, and round-shouldered. On another Wednesday she'd given him a pot belly produced by the ever-present supply of beer in his refrigerator. He'd had red hair and freckles, drab brown hair parted in the middle and slicked down with water, and on one occasion she'd added thick bifocals to complete the picture. It was an ongoing game that she played every Wednesday morning, and she thoroughly enjoyed it.

He was a slob, she mused, as she turned onto the last block leading to Timberlane Towers. What that man did to his apartment from one Wednesday to the next was a sin. Yes, he was a tall slob. He was also quite wealthy, as evidenced by his address, the expensive clothes in the walk-in closet in his bedroom, and the designer furniture throughout the apartment.

Junior liked to read mystery novels and sci-fi, used Irish Spring soap and Colgate toothpaste. His freezer was crammed with frozen dinners, while the refrigerator held little more than beer and an occasional quart of milk.

Blake Tyrone Pemberton, Jr., also liked women.

What type of woman was attracted to a Junior, Nichelle didn't know. But lipstick on shirt collars, panty hose on the bedroom floor, and once, a pair of false eyelashes on the bathroom sink proved there was no accounting for taste. Tweaky Junior was a busy boy.

Nichelle laughed softly as she mentally drew today's picture of Mr. Pemberton. He was such a twit, poor baby, under the thumb of his domineering mother. Today he had thinning dishwater-blond hair and protruding ears. The finest orthodontist money could buy hadn't corrected his overbite, and he had a weak, nearly nonexistent chin.

Shame on you, Nichelle, she scolded herself as she burst into laughter. Junior got worse every Wednesday.

She hoisted the strap of her purse higher on her shoulder, smoothed her sweatshirt down over her jeans, and flashed a dazzling smile at Henry, the doorman of Timberlane Towers.

"Ah, if it isn't the leprechaun," the uniformed man said, smiling.

"Leprechauns, Inc.," Nichelle said, matching his smile. She glanced down at the words stenciled across the front of her green sweatshirt. "I'm incorporated, you know."

"And I say, good for you. New hat?"

"It's a long story, Henry. Do you have Mr. Pemberton's key?"

Henry pulled a key ring from his pocket, extracted one, and handed it to Nichelle.

"Have a nice day," he said.

"Doing the down-and dirty," she said merrily. "See you later, Henry."

Nichelle crossed the intimidatingly elegant lobby, then rode the elevator to the fifteenth floor. She entered Junior Pemberton's apartment and placed the key on a small shelf below a mirror in the foyer. Making a fervent wish that her hair had been miraculously restored to its original color, she whisked the hat from her head and looked in the mirror.

Green.

"Yuck," she said, wrinkling her nose.

She fluffed the soft curls and decided to count her blessings. At least her hair wasn't brittle as straw or falling out in clumps. But Eric was still close to taking his last breath.

She gazed intently at her reflection, blinked her large dark eyes, then smiled to reveal her straight white teeth. What a face, she thought with a silent moan. Everyone said she was cute. Cute! At twenty-three that was *not* a compliment. She wanted words like *beautiful, sultry, sexy, sophisticated* tossed her way. What was a person to do with a face that hadn't changed since her senior picture in the high school yearbook?

She leaned closer to the mirror. Her eyes were too big, she decided. Great eyes on Bambi but . . . Her nose and mouth were nothing to write home about, either. Little nose, a couple of lips, a fairly decent chin, and it all added up to cute.

And this body. She frowned down at herself. Slim. Lord, how boring. When Marcella wore her Leprechauns, Inc. shirt, a person could hardly read the lettering because Marcella's voluptuous breasts pushed the slogan this way and that. But Nickie? Her shirt was as flat as a billboard. Terrific advertising, but rough on the morale.

"Oh, well," she said with a shrug, "maybe I'm a late bloomer. I might be a real knockout when I'm thirty."

She dumped her hat and purse on a chair in the foyer and walked into the living room. Her glance quickly surveyed the cluttered room.

"Tsk, tsk," she clucked. "What a slob you are, Junior. But fear not, the leprechaun is here." Business as usual, she mused. She'd gather the laundry and get it started in the basement laundry room, then come back up and tackle this disaster. Last week the kitchen floor had been so awful, she'd nearly stuck to it before she could get it scrubbed.

Humming softly, she crossed the living room to the hallway beyond with the intention of gathering Junior Pemberton's dirty laundry from the large master bedroom. She zoomed into the bedroom, glanced at the bed, then started toward the bathroom.

"Oh . . . my . . . God," she whispered. She came to such an abrupt halt that she nearly toppled over, then she turned slowly, very slowly, to face the bed. "Oh . . . my . . . God."

There was a man in the bed.

With the sheet pulled only to his waist, there was a half-naked man in the bed.

There was the most gorgeous, incredibly virile, half-naked man in the bed.

Nichelle drew in a gulp of air when she suddenly realized she wasn't breathing, then moved on trembling legs to the foot of the bed, staring at the sleeping man. A definite conclusion thudded against her brain: Junior Pemberton was *not* tweaky.

His thick black hair was tousled and fell onto a tanned forehead. He had rugged features—high cheekbones, a straight nose, a firm chin, and, Lord above, those lips. His gently parted lips were just begging—*begging*, Nichelle told herself—to be kissed. Strong neck, wide shoulders, and deliciously muscled arms. The best till last: that chest. Bronzed by the sun, covered in curly black hair, it was absolutely divine.

Nichelle's gaze skimmed quickly over the lower half of Junior Pemberton, covered by the sheet, and saw that he was, indeed, tall. Those were long legs beneath that sheet. She would not, she decided, dwell on the thought of what else was hidden from her view. Merciful heaven, what a man. Every picture that she'd created on previous Wednesdays was whisked into oblivion.

But what was he doing here? she wondered. *She* was here, so he was supposed to be off doing whatever he did to earn his *beaucoup* bucks. Now what? Should she leave? No, she was scheduled to be here on Wednesdays, and there was no way to juggle her schedule. Maybe if she crept around like a thief in the night, she could gather the laundry without waking beautiful Junior. Oh, that name didn't fit him. It really didn't.

Suddenly Junior moaned and shifted his head on the pillow. Nichelle went ramrod stiff. In the next instant he lunged upward to a sitting position and opened his eyes.

Her mouth dropped as their eyes met, then . . . she hit the deck! Why she did it, she wasn't sure, but she flung herself flat onto the thick carpet and covered her face with her hands, having the irrational thought that if she didn't look at Junior, he couldn't see her. Hardly breathing, she strained her ears for any sound coming from the bed. She heard a moan.

Blake Pemberton blinked once slowly, then sank back against the pillow and closed his eyes.

He was delirious, he thought, pressing his hands to his throbbing head. He knew he had a fever, but it was higher than he'd estimated. His brain was fried. He'd actually imagined seeing an alien creature with green hair standing at the foot of his bed!

"Ohhh," he groaned. He was dying. Every bone in his body ached. He was hot and then cold. But green hair? He'd seen her so clearly, then she'd disappeared. She? Yes, it had been a woman alien. A small, delicate woman with big eyes, a lovely face, and green hair! He was really sick. He couldn't remember ever having had the flu this badly. What time was it? What day was it? Oh, hell, who cared? He groaned again, then flopped his arms onto the bed with a thud.

Nichelle didn't move. With her face still pressed in her hands she lay on the floor and didn't move. Five minutes passed. Ten minutes. Then with her heart racing she pushed herself up to her hands and knees and crawled around the end of the bed and along the side. Swallowing heavily, she raised herself slowly upward until her chin cleared the mattress.

Junior Pemberton had rolled onto his side and was asleep, his face only inches from hers. A soft smile formed on her lips as she gazed at him. There was the stubble of a beard on his cheeks, and any woman would kill for his eyelashes. He was so handsome. The impact of his raw masculinity caused a funny flutter in the pit of her stomach.

He opened his eyes.

Nichelle couldn't move.

"Oh, Lord, she's back," he muttered, his voice raspy.

"Hi," she said, managing a weak smile. She pushed herself up to her knees.

"Leprechauns, Inc.," he said, staring at her sweatshirt. "Is that your name or your planet? Do you know E.T.?"

"I beg your pardon?"

"You did a mind-meld on me, right? That's how you know my language. Oh, Lord." He rolled onto his back. "Why am I talking to you? You don't even exist. Go away and let me die in peace."

Nichelle frowned and cocked her head to one side. What was he babbling about? she wondered. He sounded like a raving lunatic.

"Mr. Pemberton," she started, "I—"

He snatched the sheet and yanked it up to his throat. "I'm warning you," he said, glaring at her. "If you don't beam yourself back up to your spaceship in the next five seconds, I won't be held responsible for my actions."

"Huh?"

"Oh, Lord, I'm hot. No, I'm cold. My bones are disintegrating."

She narrowed her eyes and leaned closer to Junior

Pemberton. His face was flushed, she now realized. In spite of the stubble of beard and deep tan, she could see the unhealthy glow to his skin. His gray eyes were like soupy fog. He wasn't crazy, he was sick, had the flu or something worse. Her green hair! Oh, Lord, she thought, swallowing a bubble of laughter, he was convinced she was an illusory creature from outer space brought on by his fever. Oh, good grief, how hysterically funny.

"Mr. Pemberton," she said, unable to suppress her smile, "I think you have the flu."

"I *know* I have the flu," he said. "I'm delirious. But since I'm intelligent enough to realize that I'm delirious, the polite thing for you to do would be to disappear and let me die in peace."

"Aspirin," she said, getting to her feet. "You need aspirin to bring down that fever, and you must have liquids. Don't move, I'll be right back."

"Don't come back," he said, squeezing his eyes tightly closed. "I can't take any more of this. A man has the right to die with dignity. I don't want to check out, uttering my final words to an alien creature who doesn't even exist."

Nichelle laughed and left the room. A thorough search of the kitchen cupboards turned up a jar of orange juice powder and an unopened bottle of aspirin. She made a large pitcher of juice, poured it over ice cubes in a glass, and shook two aspirin into her hand. When she returned to the bedroom, Junior was sleeping, the sheet still pulled up to his throat, clutched tightly in his hands.

"Mr. Pemberton," she called. "Yoo-hoo, Junior, wake up."

His eyes flew open. "Junior? Junior! Don't you dare call me that. The name is Blake. You must do a lousy mind-meld or you'd know that. Listen, leprechaun, take pity on me and go away, okay?"

"Yes, I will," she said solemnly, "just as soon as you take these aspirin and drink this juice."

"That juice is an illusion."

"Humor me. You want me to transport myself out of here, don't you? Your mission, should you choose to accept it, is to swallow these pills and drink this orange juice."

"Then you'll leave?"

"I swear on the oath of an extraterrestrial being. I'll pho-o-one home," she said in a gravelly voice, "and have them zap me up."

"You've got a deal," Blake said. He pushed himself up against the headboard, then moaned. "Oh, my head." He pressed his hands to his temples and the sheet immediately slid down below his waist, revealing a narrowing strip of hair and a swirl of curl around his navel. "Give them to me, leprechaun."

"What?" she said, tearing her gaze from the enticing view. "Oh, here." She handed him the aspirin and juice.

Blake swallowed the pills and drank the juice, eyeing her warily the entire time. He shoved the glass back into her hand.

"There," he said. "Good-bye." He slid down and closed his eyes. "Are you gone?"

"I will be just as soon as I contact my ship. Well, it was nice meeting you."

"Go away!"

"Oh. Right."

In the living room Nichelle sank onto the sofa and

stifled the laughter that threatened to erupt. If she hadn't just taken part in that absurd scenario, she wouldn't have believed it had happened. It had been absolutely crazy.

In the next instant she frowned. Junior—no, Blake Pemberton—was really quite ill. He'd need more aspirin later, and a continual supply of liquids. Should she phone his mother? Somehow that didn't seem like a good idea. Mrs. Pemberton was a nervous, fluttering woman and she called her son Junior. Nichelle couldn't picture Blake wanting his mother hovering over him.

Blake Tyrone Pemberton, she mused. It was a strong, powerful name that suited the man perfectly. *Never* had she seen a male that exuded such virility, such sexuality. No wonder there was continual evidence in the apartment of visits by women. Blake probably had to beat them off with a stick. Even sick as a dog he was the best-looking man she had ever seen. Oh, what would it be like to be pulled against that muscular body, held in those strong arms, kissed by those luscious lips? She'd sink her fingers into his thick, ebony hair and—

"Nichelle Clay, shame on you," she said, jumping to her feet. She felt the warm flush on her cheeks and a tingling along her spine. This would never do, she told herself. Fantasizing about an imaginary tweaky Junior was one thing. Mentally leaping into the arms of the real-life Blake Pemberton was something else again. Enough was enough. Back to the problem at hand—what to do about the state of Blake's health.

She walked back to the bedroom door and peered

in. Blake was asleep, sprawled on his stomach. The solution, she decided, was to do her chores as scheduled, except for the noisy vacuuming, then be there when he woke up again to give him more aspirin and juice. She could only hope his fever would have dropped enough by then so he wouldn't pitch a fit when he discovered she hadn't had herself beamed aboard her spaceship. If the aspirin had worked, she'd appear as a perfectly normal woman with green hair. Grim.

She crept into the bedroom and began to pick up the clothes strewn around the floor. Blake moaned softly in his sleep and she hurried to the edge of the bed. His broad, tanned back seemed to beckon to her to touch it, to trace the steely muscles beneath the smooth skin. She tightened her hold on the clothes in her arms as a curl of heat began deep within her and whispered throughout her.

She told herself to move, to walk away, to ignore Blake Pemberton and get on with her chores, but she was riveted to the spot. Her small breasts suddenly felt heavy, achy, and a tingling sensation skittered along her spine. She swayed unsteadily, feeling like a leaf blown about by an unexpected gust of wind, unable to control its flight to an unknown place.

The clothes in her arms held the aroma of Blake, of soap and aftershave, the heady scent of perspiration, and an essence that was simply male. She had touched his garments each Wednesday for weeks, but now there was a man to envision in the jeans and shirts, the slacks and sweaters. A man who was affecting her like none before, drawing her to him like a magnet. A man who was scaring her to death.

She shook her head to clear the hazy mist that seemed to have settled over her, then spun around and nearly ran into the living room. She dumped the clothes on the sofa, then returned to scoop out the ones Blake had managed to get into the hamper and added them to the pile. After retrieving a laundry basket from the storeroom off the kitchen, she separated the dry cleaning from the washable items and set the cleaning on the parson's bench in the foyer. With a box of detergent perched on the top of the load in the laundry basket, she left the apartment and headed for the basement.

Blake slowly opened his eyes and rolled onto his back, groaning as his aching muscles protested the motion. He ran his hand down his face and took a mental inventory of how he felt. Lousy. He felt really rotten, and understood the saying about having to die to feel better.

What a crazy dream he'd had, he thought. A green-haired alien had landed in his bedroom. It had seemed so real; *she* had seemed so real. He could still hear the lilting sound of her laughter, see her lovely face and slender body. He remembered her small breasts, barely discernible under a sweatshirt that had said LEPRECHAUN. No, it had been LEPRECHAUNS, INC. He never dreamed, or if he did, he didn't remember upon awakening. But this dream? Oh, yes, he remembered the leprechaun. She was exquisite, except for the green hair, of course.

He laughed hoarsely as he realized he was spending his energy thinking about a figment of his fever-racked imagination. But she'd seemed so alive. She was tiny, and he'd have to be careful if he—

"Hell, Pemberton," he muttered, "you've got a screw loose. She flew off in her spaceship, remember?"

In his dream, he mused, the leprechaun had given him juice and aspirin. That was a direct message from his subconscious, he decided, telling him what he needed to have.

With a groan he swung his feet to the floor, then pushed himself upward, blinking as a wave of dizziness assaulted him. He glanced around for a pair of jeans to put on and frowned as he realized there were no clothes lying on the floor. Whether that made sense he wasn't sure, but he decided he didn't have the energy to think about it, or to worry about the proprieties of streaking through his own apartment.

With less than steady steps he weaved his way out of the bedroom, across the hall, and into the living room. His head was buzzing and throbbing from the effort, and he paused a moment to catch his breath.

He hated this, he thought, starting off again. He was never sick. He didn't have time for this nonsense. He'd drink juice and take aspirin by the carload so he could get back to the office, where he belonged. Oh, hell, he probably didn't have any juice and aspirin. Wonderful. Just dandy. Beer he had. Beer was a liquid. And the thought of drinking a beer was enough to make him sicker.

He made it to the kitchen, then slouched against the counter, perspiration bathing his body. His eyes widened as he realized his nose was three inches from a bottle of aspirin. He snatched it up and stared at it, then slammed it back onto the counter as though it had burned his fingers. He glanced at the refrigerator out of the corner of his eye and reached for the handle with trembling fingers.

"Beer," he said. "That's all there is in there." He pulled open the door, saw the pitcher of orange juice, and slammed the door shut. "Oh, good Lord," he whispered, "she's real. The leprechaun is real!"

Don't be ridiculous, he told himself. He had to calm down, think this through. The only logical conclusion was that he was still asleep and this was all part of his dream. But he didn't believe that for a minute. A man knew when he was wide-awake, for crying out loud.

He pressed his palm to his forehead, felt the unnatural heat of his skin, then checked his pulse. He definitely had a fever, that much he knew. So, okay, he'd had a vivid dream about a beautiful woman with green hair who had beamed down into his bedroom. Check. Then, in a state of delirium, he'd gotten up, come to the kitchen, and fixed the orange juice. Check. He'd dreamed that the leprechaun had brought him the drink and pills, but that part wasn't true. He was, and had been all along, alone in his apartment. Check.

"Oh, thank heavens," he said, sagging against the counter. "I figured it out."

He reached for the bottle of aspirin, only to stiffen, his hand halting in midair as he heard a key being inserted in the front door. The door opened, then closed. He glanced around frantically, then grabbed a hand towel off a rack and held it below his waist. Sweat trickled down his chest as he inched to the kitchen door and peered into the living room.

"Oh, no!" he yelled.

"Aaak!" Nichelle screamed, spinning around to face him. "What are you doing here?"

"What are *you* doing here? I had this all worked out, dammit."

"How dare you stand there nude," she said, planting her hands on her hips. And gorgeous beyond belief, she thought. She couldn't handle this!

"I'm not nude," he said, glancing down at the skimpy towel.

"But close to it. This is insulting." And very hard on the nervous system, she added silently. Blake Pemberton exuded such blatant sexuality, it was sinful. If she started drooling, she was going to be absolutely mortified.

He strode across the room and loomed above her. She stared up at him, her heart racing.

"I want," he said through clenched teeth, "an explanation. A reasonable explanation that does not include any reference to E.T. or spaceships. Got that?"

"An explanation," she repeated. For what? she wondered dreamily. He wanted her to think while he was standing so close to her, filling her senses with his heat and aroma? Fat chance.

"Who in the hell are you?" he asked in a very loud voice.

She jumped. "Oh, *that* explanation. I'm Leprechauns, Inc."

"I can read your chest," he muttered.

Chest? she thought. How depressing. Couldn't he have said "boobs" or "bosom." No, guess not. She definitely had a chest.

"Well?"

"Oh, it's very simple. This is Wednesday, so I'm

here. Your mother gave me to you for your birthday. I'm the leprechaun who makes this war zone spiffy clean every week. Understand?"

"You're—you're the cleaning lady?"

"That's me. I thrive on grime." She laughed. "It's a thrill a minute."

He narrowed his eyes. "Why did you pretend to be a creature from outer space?"

"I did no such thing. You told me I was, and I didn't think I should argue with someone who was ill. Are you feeling better?"

"No. Why is your hair green?"

"Oh, that." She pulled a curl around to look at it. "Eric did his homework assignment on me. Never again, I can tell you that. Kurt can be the guinea pig even if he isn't blond."

Blake shook his head as if clearing it. "I think I need to lie down."

"You do look tired. Would you like me to bring you some more juice?"

"Yeah, fine, fine," he said, moving around her and heading for the bedroom. "Whatever."

Nichelle told herself in no uncertain terms that she was not to turn her head to catch a glimpse of Blake's exit from the room. She also knew she had no intention of listening to herself. She dipped her head and took a peek. Oh, merciful saints. On top of everything else that Blake Pemberton had been dished out, he had the nicest, tightest buns she had ever seen. She really wasn't going to survive this man.

With a whimsical sigh she went into the kitchen to pour a glass of orange juice for Blake, then returned to his bedroom. She hesitated outside the open door, then finally knocked on the doorframe.

"Little late for social amenities, isn't it?" he said from the bed. "You beamed down without knocking."

"That wasn't my fault," she said, marching to the edge of the bed. "I thought that agreeing with you was the thing to do at the time. You were very ill, Mr. Pemberton. In fact, you still are."

"Blake," he said, looking directly up at her. "Call me Blake."

"Oh, well, sure. Here's your juice . . . Blake."

He pushed himself up on one elbow and accepted the glass. "What's your name, leprechaun?"

"Incorporated. I mean, my business is called Leprechauns, Inc. I'm Nichelle Clay, but most people call me Nickie."

"Nichelle," he said slowly. "Nice. Very pretty."

"Thank you, but I had nothing to do with picking it. Well, I've got to trot back down to the basement and shift your laundry from the washer to the dryer. 'Bye."

"Wait," he said, grabbing her hand.

"Yes?"

"Who're Eric and Kurt?"

"My neighbors."

"Close neighbors?"

"Right across the hall."

"That isn't what I mean. I'm trying to find out if there's a special man in your life."

"Oh, no, there isn't. I've been terribly busy getting my business off the ground the last two years. . . ." His hand was so warm, she thought frantically. The heat was traveling up her arm, across her shoulders, down to her breasts. . . . Mercy sake's. "And I haven't had time to devote to a relationship. I have six part-time employees now."

"And you all do cleaning?" he asked, stroking her wrist with his thumb. She was so small, he mused. Her hand would disappear in his, be buried, just like he wanted to bury himself inside her. Good Lord, if she could really do a mind-meld, she'd probably punch him.

"Leprechauns, Inc., does everything," she was saying. "Cleaning, shopping for groceries or gifts, baby-sitting, yardwork, you name it. We provide much-needed services for busy working people."

"I'm impressed," he said, nodding. "Do you have an office?"

"No, I work out of my apartment. Your mother heard of me through her bridge club. We grocery-shop for one of her friends."

He smiled at her. "And my mother gave you to me for my birthday."

"Relatively speaking." Oh, that smile, she thought. It lit up his feverish gray eyes and melted her right down to her socks. "Surely you've been aware that your apartment has been cleaned every Wednesday for three months."

"Yes, but I didn't know a leprechaun was doing it. That's a catchy name, and very appropriate."

"Thank you," she said, and slowly retrieved her hand. "You should rest now. I'll try not to disturb you while I do my chores."

Oh, she was disturbing him all right, he thought dryly. His libido was going crazy. It had to be the fever. Nichelle Clay was definitely not his type.

"It's about your hair," he said.

She laughed. "Isn't it awful? Eric better have a solution to this mess by the time I get home. Well, I'm off to the laundry room."

He watched as she crossed the bedroom. "Nichelle?" he said, his voice low and rumbly.

"Yes?" She stopped and turned toward him.

"I may be interested in hiring you for some of your other services."

"Such as?"

He laced his hands beneath his head and smiled up at the ceiling. "I'll lie here and give it some serious thought."

Nichelle opened her mouth, shut it again, then hurried from the room.

Two

In the laundry room Nichelle transferred the wet clothes from the washer to the dryer, then stood staring at the bright colors as they tumbled together. She envisioned her mind as being in the same jumbled disarray, and drew a steadying breath.

O-kay, she told herself, she was fine now. Just peachy-keen. She was willing to admit that Blake—gorgeous, virile Blake—had momentarily knocked her off kilter. And, yes, her body had gone a little nuts and her imagination slightly haywire while close to Blake Pemberton, but it was no big deal. So what if she was still tingling from head to toe, and the image of Blake's nearly nude body was etched with indelible ink on her brain? It didn't mean a thing.

His parting shot about possibly wanting more of her services had been a business-related statement, she decided. She'd simply read too much into the way he'd said it in that low, sexy voice of his. It stood to reason that she'd become a bit rattled upon finding a naked man in what should have been an empty bed. And it wasn't every day of the week that a person was mistaken for a green-haired alien. She was holding up quite well given the circumstances of her morning.

"I'm proud of you, Nichelle," she said aloud, and left the laundry room.

Back in the apartment she peered into the bedroom and saw that Blake was sleeping, one arm flung over his eyes. She gazed at him for a long moment, but when her heart began to thud wildly against her ribs, she spun around with a snort of disgust and stomped into the kitchen.

She washed the kitchen floor, scoured the sink, and began to polish the living room tables. She told herself that she'd totally forgotten that Blake was snoozing away in the next room, admitted she was lying through her teeth, and continued with her chores.

When an hour had passed, she returned to the laundry room to retrieve the dry clothes. She lugged the basket into the living room, then began to sort and fold the wash into neat piles.

She'd been doing this for weeks, she reminded herself. There was no reason whatsoever for the warm flush on her cheeks as she folded Blake's briefs. White briefs, dark blue, brown, black. Underwear was underwear, and his had a thirty-four waist. It made no difference that she'd seen the thirty-four inches of that waist that connected to narrow hips, that led to muscular legs. And, of course, above that waist was a chest that was a dream in itself.

"Oh, stop it," she muttered. "This is absurd."

Then she stiffened at the sound of the water running in the shower. Blake was awake and showering, she realized, but what if he got dizzy, slipped and fell, whacked his head on the tiles? He could drown in there while she was blissfully folding his underwear. Well, she couldn't exactly go charging in and stand guard while he showered. Intriguing thought, but out of the question.

Nichelle sighed. Blake Tyrone Pemberton, Jr., himself, was out of the question, she mused. Out of her league and out of her world. She belonged an hour's bus ride away, which might as well be that other planet he'd originally assumed she'd come from. Leprechauns, Inc., was doing well, she worked hard, and she was proud of her accomplishments. But it was all relative to the boundaries of her world, and it wasn't remotely close to the upper crust of Bel Air.

A sudden thought struck her and she stared straight ahead, a pair of briefs dangling from the tip of her finger. She wouldn't see Blake Pemberton again after she left his apartment today. The Wednesdays ahead would be back to business as usual. She would come and go as the unseen leprechaun that she was, out of sight, out of mind, and totally forgotten by Blake.

"I know that," she said to the underwear. So why did the thought of being in this empty apartment week after week seem so bleak, so depressing? If anything, Blake was in the way. She couldn't vacuum or change the sheets on his bed, which was messing up her routine. She could be her usual efficient self without him here. Without him here seeming to fill the rooms to overflowing with his vibrant masculinity and magnetism, with his smile that lit up his entire face.

Oh, such crazy ramblings, Nichelle scolded herself. Blake was a client, nothing more. She'd met him purely by accident under bizarre circumstances, and would never see him again. She was being honest enough to admit that he'd stirred new and startling sensations within her, but she'd chalk it up as a fascinating experience, then forget it. So be it.

"Oh, Lord," a voice said, snapping her from her reverie. She turned and saw Blake walk into the room. He sank into a chair and spread his jean-clad legs out in front of him. He was bare-chested, clean-shaven, and his thick dark hair was damp.

He was so incredibly, wonderfully male, she thought, staring at him, that she wanted to sing with joy at the mere sight of him. Her body seemed to hum with the awareness of her own femininity. She was suddenly not too slim and not too flat, but gently curved, soft and, oh, so womanly—an enticing counterpart to Blake Pemberton. The scents of soap and aftershave wafted through the air, and she filled her senses with the fresh aromas.

"Do you have a thing for my briefs?" he asked, looking at the pair dangling from her finger.

"What? Oh, no, of course not." She quickly folded them, placed them on the proper pile, then reached for a pair of jeans. "How are you feeling?"

"Not great. I thought a shower might help, but now I'm exhausted. This is the pits. I don't have time for this stupidity. My secretary is juggling all my appointments and . . . hell."

"What kind of work do you do?"

"Investments. I have some backers interested in a

big land deal I'm putting together in Texas right now. Damn, I've got to get to my office."

She scooped up a pile of clothes. "Blake, you can't rush the flu. It has to run its course. You might feel a bit better, though, if you ate something."

"Frozen dinners hold no appeal," he said gruffly. "A dying man needs real food, not wrinkled peas and greasy chicken. Or a brownie the size of a postage stamp. Or some apple crunch junk with no apples."

"Okay," Nichelle said, laughing, "I get the point. Are you going to stay up awhile? I need to wash the sheets on your bed."

"I'll have to. I'm too weak to move out of this chair. Hey, I know. I'll hire you to go get some decent food."

"Now?"

"Yeah. There's a market around the corner. Bring back enough for us to have lunch, then have the rest delivered. Good stuff. Meat, French bread, fruit, the works. Some chopped sirloin for hamburgers for lunch would be great. Can you cook?"

"Of course."

"I can't. Frozen dinners are the best I can do. Do you like hamburgers?"

"It isn't necessary for you to buy my lunch."

"I hate to eat alone. Come on, Nichelle, be a sport. I need some protein in my deteriorating body."

"Well, all right. Let me strip the bed and get another load of wash started, then I'll go to the market."

"Strip my bed?" He smiled and wiggled his eyebrows. "Sounds racy. You fold my briefs, strip my bed. What other intimate things do you do for me around here that I'm not aware of?"

"Clean your grungy shaving cream out of the bathroom sink." She frowned. "If you ever decide to marry, you owe it to your wife to warn her that you're not Mr. Neat."

He pushed himself to his feet. "I don't intend to get married. I'll get you some money for the groceries."

"No, I guess there's no reason for you to marry," she said, following him into the bedroom with a load of clean laundry. "I'll put these clothes away."

He took his wallet from the top of the dresser and extracted several bills. She opened the top drawer and placed his underwear inside.

"Ah-ha," he said. "The lady goes into my drawers. Think of the headlines. 'Nichelle Clay is in Blake Pemberton's drawers every Wednesday.' Tongues would wag, my dear."

"You're sick," she said.

"That's what I've been trying to tell you. I need food. What do you mean, I'd have no reason to marry?"

"You're a little slow on the uptake too. I was referring to the fact that you obviously aren't lacking in female companionship."

"How in the hell do you know that?"

"Panty hose, false eyelashes, lipstick on shirts. How did Miss Six-and-a-half-narrow get home without her shoes?"

He shrugged. "Beats me. I didn't know that someone had left her shoes here."

She began to pull the sheets off the bed. "I put them in your closet last week."

"Oh." He frowned and rested his arms on the top of the dresser. "You certainly seem to know an awful lot about me. It's rather disconcerting."

She scooped up the sheets and headed for the door. "Your secrets are safe with me," she said over her shoulder.

"Hey," he said, following close behind, "you make me sound like a pervert or something."

She laughed. "Don't be silly." She dumped the sheets into the laundry basket, then went into the foyer for her hat. "I just assume that you wouldn't want the frequency of your female friends' visits or the color of your underwear discussed beyond these walls."

"You know more about me than my own mother does," he said, then groaned. "Oh, my head."

"Why don't you take two more aspirin and stretch out on the sofa while I'm gone. You've been up too long."

"Now you *sound* like my mother," he muttered. "Or a naggy wife."

"Well, I do things around here that some wives would do," she said, accepting the money he slapped into her hand. "I pick up after you, wash your clothes, scrub the floors."

"Oh, yeah?" He suddenly grinned. "Just how far are you willing to go in your wifely duties?"

"Well," she said, batting her eyelashes, "I draw the line at nagging. 'Bye." She plopped her hat on her head, grabbed the laundry basket, and started for the door. "Take two aspirin and lie down . . . Junior," she said as her parting shot.

Blake chuckled and shook his head as the door closed behind Nichelle. He walked slowly into the kitchen, poured himself a glass of orange juice, and swallowed two aspirin. He leaned against the counter as he sipped the remaining juice.

Nichelle Clay was feisty, he mused. Cute as a button too. He had to admire her for creating Leprechauns, Inc., and making a go of it. It wasn't easy getting a new business off the ground.

As his head began spinning again he went back into the living room and stretched out on the sofa. He hoped he recovered from his dread disease. Hell, he hoped he didn't croak by midnight. He closed his eyes, but in the next instant they popped open again.

Who in the hell had left their shoes in his bedroom? he wondered. Clare? Suzanne? Did he care? Not really. They were all party-hardy gals who liked to go first class and have a good time, and who weren't interested in commitments or serious relationships. That suited him perfectly. But, dammit, he didn't like the idea that Nichelle thought he was some kind of sex maniac. He didn't have a woman in his bed every night of the week, for cripe's sake.

Nichelle, he thought, closing his eyes again. Pretty name. And she was lovely. He was eager to see her when her hair was blond instead of green. But when would he see her again? Well, hell, he'd ask her out for dinner. No, he wouldn't, because he had a feeling in the pit of his stomach that she'd turn him down flat. Nichelle wouldn't go out with a fast-lane hustler, and he was a fast-lane hustler from the word go. And she knew it.

He didn't like this, he decided. He definitely didn't like the fact that Nichelle had been keeping tabs on his sex life, folding his underwear, going into his drawers for the past three months. It was an invasion of his privacy. Worse yet, he felt compelled to apologize because Miss Six-and-a-half-narrow had left her shoes on his bedroom floor. Dammit, no. He didn't owe Nichelle any explanations for the way he conducted his life. She was, after all, the hired help.

"That stinks, Pemberton," he muttered. She was, in actuality, a beautiful young woman who owned a unique business that was apparently doing very well. She was independent, intelligent, and willing to work hard. She was attractive in a fresh, wholesome way, unlike the glitzy women he went out with. She had a great sense of humor and looked him right in the eye when she spoke to him.

And he wanted her.

There it was, the bottom line. He wanted Nichelle Clay.

Blake groaned and ran his hand down his face. Why? he asked himself. Why did he have this ache in his gut that told him he wanted to make love with Nichelle? He barely knew her. Her lack of worldliness and sophistication would no doubt carry over into the bedroom. She wasn't at all like the experienced, voluptuous women he usually took to his bed.

But, dammit, he wanted her.

She made him feel alive, vital, despite his illness. He would have to be gentle with her, teaching her the mysteries of his body and learning the same about hers. He'd do nothing to frighten her. He would please her first, before seeking his own gratification. It would be heaven.

He was assuming a lot, he supposed, by deciding that Nichelle knew little of men. But he sensed an innocence and honesty that radiated from her. He'd been alarmed when she'd mentioned Eric and Kurt, not liking the idea that she might be involved with other men.

Strange sentiments for him, Blake mused. Maybe his sudden, unexpected attraction to Nichelle was due to the fact that he had a fever and wasn't thinking clearly. Yes, that was probably what this was all about. He'd keep out of her way when she got back and forget the whole damn thing.

"Fine," he said, and rolled over onto his stomach.

Nichelle was having a marvelous time.

She'd grocery-shopped for Leprechauns, Inc., clients before, but had always been given a list of precisely what to buy. For Blake it was different. She was determined to stock his kitchen with healthful foods, yet keep everything simple enough for him to prepare, even though he claimed he couldn't cook. Anyone could scramble an egg.

She began to fill a bag with peaches, rejecting more than she accepted as not being perfect enough. What she had said to Blake was true, she realized. The chores she'd been performing for him over the past weeks were those of a traditional wife. She cleaned his home, washed his clothes, left him notes to remind him when he was running low on shaving cream or soap. And now she was shopping for his food. None of it had seemed significant when he'd been an imaginary Junior. But now he was Blake.

She was thinking such foolish thoughts, she told herself. She was a leprechaun, not a wife. She'd been hired to perform manual labor. The real wifely duties, the intimate, sexual ones, were taken care of by Blake's endless string of women.

Nichelle wrinkled her nose, thudded a peach into the bag, and moved on to the bin of oranges.

• • •

Blake had drifted into a light sleep when he heard the key being inserted in the door. He sat up and stretched his aching muscles as Nichelle entered the foyer. She was carrying two bags and pushed the door closed with her bottom. He hurried over to her.

"Let me take those," he said. Oh, hell, look at her, he thought. She was gazing up at him with those big brown eyes from beneath the brim of that crazy hat. So much for staying out of her way. Maybe she really was a leprechaun, and was weaving a magical spell over him.

"Thank you," she said.

"For what?"

"For offering to help. You take one bag, and I'll carry the other."

"Oh, no, I'll get them both." He slid his arms around the bags, and his knuckles grazed her breasts. Their eyes met as he slowly lifted the bags from her arms.

For a seemingly endless moment they simply stood there, staring at each other. Blake's gray eyes were still glazed from his fever, Nichelle thought, but she could see more in those foggy pools now. She saw desire, and her heart began to race. She told herself to go into the kitchen, but her feet ignored the directive from her brain. So she remained, feeling as though she were drowning in the misty gray of Blake's eyes.

"Do you . . . um, like peaches?" she asked, breathlessly.

"Peaches are nice," he said, his voice husky.

"Good, because I bought peaches."

"I'm sure they're great."

"I hope so."

This was the dumbest conversation he'd even taken part in, Blake thought suddenly. He tore his gaze from Nichelle's and peered into one of the bags. "First-rate peaches," he said, then spun around and strode into the kitchen.

Nichelle tossed her hat onto the chair in the foyer and followed him into the kitchen. He was pulling things out of one of the bags and tossing them onto the counter. When the peaches landed with a soft thud, she cringed but kept her mouth shut as she took the groceries from the other bag. When their arms brushed against each other she swallowed heavily.

There was nothing intimate, she told herself firmly, about unloading grocery sacks with a man. Eggs and oranges, macaroni and cheese, were not erotic. But, oh, Blake smelled so good, and she could feel the heat of his tempting body. That heat seemed to travel throughout her like tiny, feathery fingers. She had to think about something else!

"Are you feeling any better?" she asked, not looking at him.

"I guess so."

"Did you take some more aspirin?"

"Yeah. You told me to, so I did."

Why that pleased Nichelle right down to her toes she wasn't sure, but she knew there was a bright smile on her face when she looked up at him.

"I'll fix lunch," she said. "You rest and I'll call you when it's ready."

"I'll sit over here." He slouched onto a chair at the kitchen table.

"There? Wouldn't you be more comfortable on the

sofa? I put your sheets into the dryer when I came back, but they wouldn't be dry yet. You really should consider buying an extra set. You're going to need a new floor mop soon too. Oh, and some sponges and—"

"Nichelle."

"Would you like me to make you a list so you'll know what—"

"Nichelle."

"Yes?"

"Do I make you nervous?"

"Nervous?" she squeaked.

He laced his fingers behind his head and smiled at her. "Nervous. You're talking a hundred miles an hour. If it'll make you feel any better, I'll admit that *you* make *me* nervous."

She burst into laughter. "Now, that is the most ridiculous thing I've ever heard."

He stood up and slowly walked toward her. "Why?"

She backed up a step. "Well, because you're you and . . . I'm me. That is, you're accustomed to being in this apartment with a woman, but I've never been here with a man. Does that make sense? Probably not. You see, I didn't expect you to be here but, son-of-a-gun, here you are."

"Yes, I am." He closed the distance between them. "And if I don't kiss you within the next five seconds, my death will be on your conscience. I really do need to kiss you, Nichelle."

"You do?" she asked, hardly breathing.

"I do."

And he did.

He cradled her face in his large warm hands and lowered his head to hers with such agonizing slowness, she was sure she was going to dissolve into a heap on the floor.

Then at last, *at last,* he covered her lips with his. Her eyes drifted closed and a soft sigh of pleasure caught in her throat. Her hands floated up to his chest, her fingers tangling in the moist curly hair and tracing the taut muscles. She explored higher, her arms circling his neck, his dropping to her back, and the kiss intensified.

Blake nestled her close to him, savoring her taste, her aroma, the gentle curves of her body. She fit so perfectly against him. He filled his senses with all that was Nichelle, and had the irrational thought that the kiss should never end. His desire for her pounded into his brain, and his manhood pressed heavily against the zipper of his jeans. His breathing became rough, and he lifted his head to drag air into his lungs.

"So sweet," he murmured, and trailed nibbling kisses down the side of her neck. "You taste so good, smell so good."

"Mr. Bubble," she said, slowly lifting her lashes.

"Hmm?"

"I use Mr. Bubble in my bath."

He chuckled and looked down at her. "You're kidding."

"No. It makes oodles of bubbles and smells terrific."

"You're really something, Nichelle Clay. And that was one helluva kiss we just shared. What are you doing to me, leprechaun?"

"I'm fixing your lunch," she said, stepping back.

"You're not angry about the kiss, are you?"

She shook her head and began to put groceries into the cupboard. Angry? she repeated silently. No, not angry. She felt . . . sad. She had never experienced a kiss like that one, never felt so wonderfully alive, feminine, even beautiful. But she was sad because the kiss had been a stolen moment in time. She had stepped over a line into a world where she didn't belong, and she couldn't, wouldn't do it again. She had no desire to become a part of Blake Pemberton's fast-moving life. She would not be one more in his endless string of women. After today she would never see him again. But, oh, it really was sad.

"Hey," he said, running his thumb over her cheek, "you look like you're about to cry. Talk to me, Nichelle. What's wrong?"

"Nothing." She seasoned the chopped sirloin, molded it into patties, then set two in a frying pan. "Blake, could you move a bit? I need to wash all this fruit."

Blake walked back to the table and sat down, a deep frown on his face. Damn, he felt like the villain in a bad movie. All he'd done was kiss Nichelle, and she'd kissed him back. Lord, had she ever. There was a lot of passion in that little package. So why did she look so stricken, as though he'd tried to ravish her in the stainless steel sink or something?

He drummed his fingers on the table and watched as she moved around the kitchen. He wanted to say something witty and clever to bring the smile back to her face, but couldn't think of anything. That had been a fantastic kiss, he fumed, and she'd enjoyed it. She had no right to look as if she just lost her best friend.

"Dammit," he said, smacking the table with his hand, "knock it off."

Nichelle jumped and three oranges rolled off the counter and onto the floor.

"What is your problem?" she asked, retrieving the fruit.

"Don't try to lay a guilt trip on me for kissing you," he said none too quietly. "You were an equal partner in that kiss, and you know it. And furthermore, that was without a doubt the most incredible kiss I have ever shared. You fit next to me like a custom-made leprechaun, and I think Mr. Bubble smells nicer than hundred-dollar-an-ounce perfume. And you enjoyed that kiss as I did, so, I repeat, knock off the Gloomy Gus routine."

She smiled. His frown deepened.

"You're right," she said, nodding. "It was a great kiss. Mind-boggling, in fact. And, yes, I was a willing participant. Since it's the only one we'll share, I think I'll cherish the memory of it."

"Hold it," he said, raising his hand. "Back up here. Why is it the only kiss we'll share?"

She flipped the hamburger. "Because I'm not going to kiss you again."

"Why the hell not?"

"You certainly yell a lot, Blake," she said. She carried plates and silverware to the table, then placed the bowl of fruit in the center. "Do you want your hamburger bun warmed?"

"I don't care. Answer the question."

"Which one?"

He clenched his jaw. "The kiss question."

"Oh, well, because it wouldn't be a good idea. You're a sensational kisser, Blake. You wouldn't believe the way I felt when you kissed me. Well, I suppose you would because you're very experienced about these things. Anyway, I know when I'm treading in dangerous waters and I have enough sense to get out. Hence, no more kisses. Get it?"

"You think I'm dangerous? That's not a very nice thing to say."

"You don't understand," she said, setting their buns in the toaster oven.

"Try me."

"I don't intend to tell you my life history, Blake. Just accept the fact that I don't intend to kiss you again." She heard a sound from the foyer. "Is that your intercom? It's probably the rest of the groceries being delivered."

"I'll answer it," he said, getting to his feet. "This discussion isn't over, Nichelle."

"Yes, it is."

He glared at her, then left the room. By the time he had waited for the delivery boy to ride up in the elevator and hand him a box of groceries, Nichelle had the lunch on the table. Blake placed the box on the counter, then they sat down and ate in silence for several minutes.

"It's delicious," he said finally.

"Thank you. I'll get your bed made up after I finish here and you can rest. Then I'll complete my chores and be on my way."

"I'd like to see you again, Nichelle," he said quietly.

She stared at her plate. "No."

"You're just going to disappear? Walk out of my life?"

"Leprechauns do that," she said, looking up at him with a small smile. "They're here, then . . . poof . . . they're gone."

"But in addition to being a leprechaun you're also

a woman. A very desirable, enchanting woman, and I want to see you again."

"No."

"Dammit, Nichelle, you're not being fair. I don't end up in bed with every woman I go out with. I'm talking about dinner, not a roll in the hay. What's wrong with spending a pleasant evening together?"

She narrowed her eyes and stared at him.

This was nuts, he thought, fuming. Why was he pleading his case like a frantic kid? He certainly wasn't lacking in dates for any night he chose, and the majority of those women were very willing to end the evening in his bed. Why was he wasting his time over a green-haired girl who was freaking out about one kiss?

Because, he admitted to himself, it *had* been a kiss like none before. He didn't know why, but he wanted the chance to find out all there was to discover about Nichelle. He was going to have to play his cards right or he'd blow it. He wanted her, he intended to have her, but the key phrase was "slow and easy."

"Dinner?" he asked. "Friday night? I won't even kiss you good night without asking permission first. I'll be the original boy scout, a real prince of a gentleman."

She laughed. "You're overdoing it."

"Seven o'clock?"

"Oh, Blake." She sighed. "This is crazy. We have nothing in common. Miss Six-and-a-half-narrow is more your type."

"Forget about her. You and I are going to relax and talk while eating a delicious dinner. That's it. Doesn't sound very dangerous to me."

"No, it doesn't."

"So?"

"Well, I . . . yes, all right."

"You could smile, you know. You look like you've just been told you have to have a root canal."

She laughed again and carried her plate to the sink. The knot in her stomach told her she'd made a mistake in agreeing to go out with Blake Pemberton. She should turn around and tell him she'd changed her mind. But she wasn't going to, and she knew it.

Blake was right, she decided. There was nothing dangerous about going to dinner. When she stuck to her guns and bid him adieu at her door, that would be the last she'd see of him. She had no idea why he was being so insistent that she go out with him, but a few more stolen hours wouldn't hurt.

"I'll go get your sheets," she said. "Then you really should go back to bed."

He smiled. "Whatever you say. When a beautiful woman orders me into bed, I do as I'm told."

She rolled her eyes heavenward and marched from the room.

Two hours later Nichelle stood at the foot of Blake's bed and watched him sleep. Still clad in his jeans, he'd collapsed onto the fresh sheets moments after she had pulled them into place. He'd mumbled something about just resting his eyes, then had fallen deeply asleep. She'd cleaned the kitchen and bathroom, organized the new supply of food, and given up on the idea of vacuuming.

There was no further reason for her to stay, and her hat was securely on her head. She was leaving.

Right now. But she didn't move. Her fingers drifted to her lips as she relived the kiss she'd shared with Blake, and she felt the now-familiar warmth creep through her. She really shouldn't go out with this man, she told herself, then added up the hours until it would be seven o'clock on Friday night.

"Sleep well, Blake Pemberton," she said softly, then turned and walked slowly from the room.

Downstairs she returned the key to Henry, bid him a cheerful good-bye, and started her trek to the bus stop. Before she had gone a block, huge drops of rain began to fall, soaking her to the skin within minutes. She sighed and continued on at her leisurely pace, deciding that dashing for cover would serve no purpose. The straw hat grew heavy with water and flopped over into her eyes, making it impossible to see.

"Darn it," she said. She snatched it off her head, then stared at the inside of it. "It's green." She ran her hand through her hair, then looked at her green fingers. "Now it comes off? Oh, Eric, you really are a dead man."

Three

When Nichelle got home and looked at herself in the mirror, she had a fit of the giggles. If Blake had decided she was an alien creature *before*, she thought merrily, he should see her now. She had a green face!

The dye had run in rivers, making an unsightly mess of her face and neck, then soaking into her sweatshirt. The people on the bus had simply pretended she wasn't there, and she had sat with a pleasant smile on her face and her hands folded primly in her lap. The driver had eyed her warily so many times in the rearview mirror, she had finally waggled her fingers at him in a friendly greeting. She had toyed with the idea of making a loud announcement that she needed to "pho-o-one home," but decided the driver might toss her out into a mud puddle.

Why the green dye had suddenly decided to relinquish its claim on her hair, she didn't know. But she was eternally grateful, and stepped into the shower with a sigh of relief. Not only would she emerge a normal color, but she'd be warm. The sudden rain had left her chilled to the bone.

If she'd caught a cold, she'd scream, she thought as she dried with a fluffy towel. She didn't have time to be sick. She'd strolled along in the downpour without a single qualm and, like an idiot, she'd kissed the living daylights out of a virus-laden man.

"Swell," she said. Now she was thinking about Blake Pemberton. She'd managed to push him from her mind during the entire soggy, hysterically funny bus ride, but now here he was in her bathroom while she was stark naked.

She stomped into the bedroom and put on clean underwear, jeans, and an enormous football jersey. She rummaged through her drawer and found the argyle socks that Eric's aunt had knitted him and he refused to wear, and pulled them onto her feet.

There, she was warm. Or she would be as soon as she blow-dried her hair.

With another sigh of relief she watched her soft blond curls fall into place as she dried them. Her hair appeared no worse for having been green. There were not, apparently, going to be any far-reaching aftereffects from the green event.

But, she mused, what about the far-reaching aftereffects from having shared an indescribably wonderful kiss with Blake Pemberton?

Nichelle walked slowly into her small yellow and white kitchen and put on a kettle of water for tea.

Visions of Blake spun in her mind, and he seemed close enough to touch. Vivid memories of his special aroma, the steely muscles of his arms, the feel of his soft lips meeting hers assaulted her, and desire hummed deep within her. A tingle of excitement rushed through her, followed by a flash of fear, and she ordered Blake to exit her brain. He didn't budge.

So much for mind-melds, she thought with a sigh. He'd taken up permanent residence in her mental space. No, darn it, this would never do. She would not become obsessed with Blake. Not with the man, nor with the remembrance of that fantastic kiss. She wouldn't think about him again until it was time to get ready for their dinner-date Friday night. Oh, ha. She was such a liar, it was a crime.

Shaking her head in disgust, she dunked a tea bag into a mug of hot water, then carried the drink to the desk in the corner of her living room. She sat down, then picked up the phone and called her answering service.

"Leprechauns, Inc.," a cheerful voice said.

"Hi, Karen. It's Nickie."

"Hi, Nickie. Ready for your messages?"

Nichelle picked up a pen. "Proceed, my dear."

"Okay, let's see. Your leprechauns have been busy. Marcella finished cleaning and shopping for Mrs. Fisher. Betsy had all the arrangements completed for the Campbells' daughter's birthday party Saturday. Brian did the yardwork at the Madisons' and walked their six poodles. Got all that?"

"Yep."

"Now then, what else? A Mrs. St. John called. She

said you have her number. She's back from Europe and wants to be put on her same schedule for cleaning and grocery-shopping, but wants to add having some meals prepared and put in the freezer each week so she doesn't have to cook."

"That's Debbie's specialty," Nichelle said.

"Mrs. Chamberlain's four grandchildren are coming for spring break from school. She'd like some organized activities planned for them because they drive her nuts. She wants a leprechaun to call her."

"Got it."

"One more. It came in just before you called me. A Mr. Blake Pemberton wishes to know when he should take more aspirin."

Nichelle sat bolt upright. "What?"

"Oh, Nickie, that man had the sexiest voice I've ever heard. I had goose bumps from head to toe. Is he gorgeous in person?"

"Well, he . . . well . . . do you have a phone number?" Nichelle could feel the warm flush on her cheeks.

"What? Oh, sure. Ready?"

"Yes, go ahead." She wrote down the telephone number that Karen gave her. "Okay, thanks. I'll talk to you later."

"Wait. Tell me more about Blake Pemberton."

"Nothing to tell," Nichelle said quickly. "Gotta go. 'Bye."

She hung up, then stared at the message, her heart racing. Blake wanted to know when to take more aspirin? That was ridiculous. All he had to do was read the instructions on the back of the bottle. He was a grown man, not a helpless child. Lord, was he ever a grown man. Well, she had no intention of returning his call.

She picked up the phone.

Anyone with half a brain could read a label on a bottle.

She dialed the number.

She didn't have time for this nonsense, she fumed.

The telephone rang on the other end and she jumped.

" 'Lo?" a voice mumbled.

"Blake? This is Nickie. I'm returning your call."

"Hello, Nichelle."

Oh, damn, she thought, moaning. Why had Karen commented on his sexy voice? *She* knew he had a sexy voice, but now that Karen had mentioned his sexy voice, it seemed even sexier.

"You weren't here when I woke up," he said.

Nichelle decided he sounded like a pouting four-year-old. "I finished my chores, except for the vacuuming."

"Well, I thought you'd at least say good-bye. Nichelle, I feel worse. I'm really sick. Should I take some more aspirin?"

"Blake, I can't really advise you about medical matters. Leprechauns, Inc., isn't licensed for that."

"I'm not asking the leprechaun, I'm asking Nichelle, the woman."

"Oh," she said weakly.

"I've had a relapse since you left me. A man needs a woman's touch at a time like this. Couldn't you come back over here and talk to me?"

She smiled. "No, Blake. Listen, you take aspirin every four hours, but I'm not sure what time you had those others. Wait another hour just to be safe."

"I'll be dead by then! Have you no heart? You're going to leave me here alone to watch my life pass before my eyes?"

She laughed. "I'm sure it will be a fascinating movie."

"You're cold, really cold."

"Go eat a peach and drink some juice."

Blake sighed. "Okay, I know when I'm being deserted. Some birthday present you are. I'll just lie here in the dark, all alone, feeling the strength ebb from my body. It doesn't matter. No one ever said life was fair."

She rolled her eyes. "Would you stop? You only have the flu, not the bubonic plague. Call your mother and ask her to come over."

"Good Lord, no! She'd pour gallons of chicken soup down me and drive me nuts." He sighed again. "I'll just tough it out on my own."

"You've very brave."

"Thank you. Are you sure you won't come back over here?"

"I'm positive."

"Well, damn. I have to hang up now, Nichelle, because I don't have the energy to hold this receiver. It's slipping from my lifeless fingers."

She chuckled. "You're a phony, Blake Pemberton."

"I am not! Well, good-bye. I'll see you Friday night."

"Are you sure you'll still be alive?"

"No, but I'll give it my best shot. You're going to feel really rotten if I die because you wouldn't come hold my hand. You'll spend the rest of your life on a massive guilt trip."

"Good-bye, Blake."

"Yeah, okay. Nichelle?"

"Yes?"

"If I had to get the flu, I'm glad it was on a Wednesday. It was nice having you here. 'Bye."

"Good-bye," she said softly, then slowly replaced the receiver. And it had been nice being there, she silently added. "Nice" did not come remotely close to describing the ecstasy of being held by Blake, kissed by Blake, seeing his devastating smile. She wanted to fly out the door, jump on a bus, and go care for him while he was ill. She'd fix his dinner, fluff the pillows on his bed, make sure he had what he needed.

What he needed? she repeated. The needs and wants of a virile man like Blake were out of her scope of experience. He'd much rather have a worldly woman like Miss Six-and-a-half-narrow. No, she couldn't meet Blake's needs. Not ever.

With a sigh Nichelle pushed every lingering detail of Blake Pemberton from her mind, and concentrated on Leprechauns, Inc.

Four of her part-time employees were students at UCLA, one was a young mother, and one was an older, widowed woman, who specialized in child care. Nichelle coordinated the assignments between the leprechauns' varying schedules with her natural flair for organization. She, herself, now spent less and less time doing the jobs, and more hours tending to the paperwork involved in running the corporation.

The fact that she cleaned Blake Pemberton's apartment each Wednesday was due to Mrs. Pemberton's powers of persuasion. Blake's mother had insisted that the president of the firm be in charge of the job.

Nichelle worked steadily through the evening, calculating hours, typing bills, tracking down leprechauns to give them the new assignments that Karen had relayed to her. Everything was under control, and finally Nichelle nodded with satisfaction at the ever-growing balance in her bank account.

Security, she mused, running her fingertip over the figures. That sum said she'd have a roof over her head and food on the table. If she worked hard and kept a sensible head on her shoulders, she'd be fine. She mustn't get illusions of grandeur, mustn't try to be what she wasn't or attempt to enter a world where she didn't belong.

Blake, she thought suddenly. He was everything she wasn't. He was dangerous because of who he was, where he lived, his entire world. And he was dangerous because when he had kissed her, she hadn't cared about anything except that kiss. She shouldn't have agreed to go out with him Friday night. She'd cancel the date.

But then she reconsidered. She could handle it, she decided, getting to her feet. She'd mentally catalogue the evening under stolen hours, just as she'd labeled the kiss a stolen moment. Yes, she'd go to dinner with Blake, then never see him again. Never ever again.

As she walked across the room toward the kitchen with thoughts of dinner, a knock sounded at her door. She opened it to a smiling Eric.

"Hi, sweetheart," he said. "I heard that—hey, your hair isn't green."

"No thanks to you," she said, spinning around and marching into the kitchen.

Eric closed the door and followed her.

"I'm sorry, Nickie," he said. "I don't know what went wrong. I still can't figure out why your hair turned green. Kurt said you were ready to kill me."

She opened the refrigerator. "I was."

"Green hair is very in at the club."

"I don't go to that place where you flex your muscles like a thug," she said, placing a head of lettuce and a tomato on the counter.

"I'm not a thug, I'm a bouncer."

"You're a six-foot-six-inch blond teddy bear," she said, laughing.

"Yeah, well." He shrugged. "I look tough. That job and delivering for the grocery store are only temporary until I get my beautician's license. Kurt is due for a raise at the radio station, so we're doing all right. Are you still mad at me?"

She smiled as she tore lettuce into a bowl.

"No."

"Good."

"However, you'll never again touch my hair."

"Have you no faith?"

"No!"

"I'm going to be a great beautician, Nickie, you'll see. Hold it, kid. A salad isn't enough for dinner. Kurt and I have lectured you thoroughly on eating properly. That rabbit food isn't going to cut it."

"I had a big lunch," she said, sitting down at the table. "Want some?"

"No, thanks. I just had four hamburgers. Listen, want to go to the UCLA basketball game with me

Friday night? Kurt has the late shift at the station again." He sat down in the chair opposite her, which looked barely capable of supporting his muscular body.

"I can't. I have a date."

"Oh?" He crossed his arms over his massive chest. "Jason?"

"No."

"Bob? Oh, I know. That guy from the pet store, Donald Duck."

"Don Duckworth," she corrected him, "but no, it's not Don or Bob. It's no one you know. Want something to drink?"

"No. Who is this guy?"

"There's a piece of chocolate cake left."

Eric leaned forward and rested his arms on the table. "Nickie, that lettuce isn't fascinating enough to stare at it like that. Look at me and tell me who you're going out with Friday night."

She peered up at him with one eye. "Blake Pemberton."

"And? Where did you meet him?"

In his bed, she thought giddily. Oh, good Lord, Eric would come unglued. It was going to be bad enough when she said, "He's a client of Leprechauns, Inc."

"What!" Eric roared. Nichelle cringed. "You're going out with someone who can afford a leprechaun? Where does he live?"

"Bel Air," she said with a sigh. "Eric, please don't yell. You'll crack the plaster on the ceiling. I know I said I'd never go out with a client because anyone who can hire a leprechaun is out of my league. But it's only a dinner-date, and I don't intend to see Blake again after Friday night."

"I don't like it," Eric said crossly. "Cancel. Go out with Donald Duck. No, go to the basketball game with me and forget this Pemberton dude. Bel Air? Jeez. Megabucks. Kurt is going to pitch a fit when I tell him."

"Then don't tell him. Having one big-brother type screaming in my face is enough, thank you very much."

"Oh, Nickie," Eric said, capturing her hand between his two enormous ones, "we *do* love you like a sister. Kurt and I would do anything for you, you know that. In the three years since you moved into the building, you've come to mean the world to us."

"And I love you guys. I don't know what I would have done without you when I first moved in."

"You came here crying, Nickie," he said gently, "and then you learned to smile again. Pemberton, Bel Air, that whole scene is wrong for you. You made a promise to yourself that you'd never cross over that invisible line between us and them."

"It's just dinner, Eric. Believe me, I have no intention of getting caught up in a world I detest. I know firsthand that it's not what I want. I'm happy right here. Trust me, okay?"

"You, I trust. Pemberton is a candidate for a broken face."

"You wouldn't hurt a flea."

"For you I would. I spent a night in jail when that yo-yo tried to hit on Kurt, didn't I? I protect my own, Nickie."

"That never did make sense," she said, shaking

her head. "Kurt is six-two and has muscles on his muscles. He can take care of himself."

"It was the principle of the thing. You, however, are a different story. You're a midget."

"I am not!"

"Give me a rundown on Pemberton. Height?"

"I don't know." She shrugged. "Six feet, maybe six-one."

"Build?"

Beautiful, she thought dreamily. Steely, bronzed, perfectly proportioned . . . beautiful. "I didn't pay that much attention," she said, poking her fork in her lettuce. "He has a nice physique, I guess."

"Good-looking?"

Incredible. Absolutely incredible. "I suppose."

"I don't like this, Nickie. Not one damn bit."

"Eric, it's only a dinner-date. Go bounce some bad guys out of the club. I adore you to pieces, but you're starting to sound like a mother hen. Good-bye."

Eric heaved himself to his feet. "You're going to give me an ulcer. I have a very sensitive stomach, you know. I can't handle stress."

"Then don't worry about me," she said, smiling. "I'll be fine Friday night."

"Hell," he said, then stalked to the door. He slammed it shut with such force that a picture on the kitchen wall tilted.

"Goodness," Nichelle said, "he's really upset." And the crummy part was, she admitted, Eric was right. She had no business going out with Blake Pemberton.

With a sigh she decided that she really had no appetite for her rabbit food after all.

• • •

At midnight Blake Pemberton was sprawled in a chair in front of the picture window in his living room, staring out over the twinkling lights of the busy city.

He had slept the evening away and was now wide awake. He was also feeling better, the aching in his muscles and throbbing in his head having subsided at last. Now he was restless, bursting with a need to do something to work off his pent-up energy.

And he was getting angrier by the minute because of Nichelle. She wouldn't leave him alone, he fumed. There she was, flitting through his mind with her smile, her big dark eyes, and that ridiculous green hair. The remembrance of their kiss was haunting him—the taste of her, the feel of her breasts, her slender body pressed against him. The memory of her laughter filled the room, then vanished, leaving the entire apartment empty and quiet. Too quiet.

Blake groaned and ran his hand over his face. He'd called Nichelle earlier on the pretense of asking when he should take his aspirin, hoping she just might consent to come back to his apartment for the evening. He hadn't really expected her to agree, yet had been surprised at how disappointed he'd felt when she refused.

Dammit, what was it about her?

The need to make love to Nichelle was consuming him, he realized. Even now, merely by envisioning her in his mind, his manhood was stirring with desire. He could see himself removing her clothes, touching and kissing every inch of her until she was whispering his name in a voice breathless with passion. Oh, he would make it good for her, teach her everything about the ecstasy they would share.

"Damn," he muttered, shifting in his chair. This was crazy. It was also rather unsettling. He could pick up the phone and select a willing partner to ease the sexual ache of his body. But he wanted Nichelle! No one else, just her. Dammit, why?

She wasn't his type, not in looks, or build, or sophistication. She was walking trouble because she didn't know the rules of playing the singles' dating game. She was everything he'd always steered clear of—and he wanted her like he'd never wanted a woman before.

He walked into his bedroom and flung himself across the bed. The sheets were twisted and tangled from his restless sleep, and he swore under his breath as he attempted to get comfortable. If Nichelle were there, he thought, she'd straighten the sheets, fluff the pillows, and . . . If Nichelle were there, he'd make love to her until dawn.

He yanked on the top sheet, then cut loose with a string of expletives as it came loose from the foot of the bed and floated over him like a parachute. He flung it onto the floor, then sank back against the pillow.

Friday night, he decided firmly, was going to be the quickest dinner-date on record. He'd be the gentleman he'd promised to be, take her to an expensive restaurant, then dump her back home before she knew what hit her. All bets were off. He had no intention of pursuing her, luring her into his bed, nothing. He wanted that leprechaun out of his head and out of his life.

"Fine," he said, then rolled onto his stomach and punched his pillow. "Ah, hell. Where's the pillowcase?"

On Friday evening Nichelle stared at her reflection in the full-length mirror in her bedroom. Her bright floral-print rayon challis skirt fell in soft folds to just a few inches above her ankles and was topped by a red nubby-textured sweater. Her strappy high-heeled shoes added three inches to her height, and her hair was a soft halo of curls around her face. Her outfit was trendy and "in," her smile forced but passable.

She did not want to go out with Blake Pemberton!

She'd seen enough of him already, she thought dryly. He'd invaded her dreams at night and stayed in her mind's eye during the day. He'd become a total nuisance, wreaking havoc with her usual efficient, organized schedule. She wanted to get this date over with as quickly as possible, and close the door on Blake forever.

She heard a knock. She took a deep breath, let it out slowly, then walked into her living room. She opened the door, and the smile on her lips instantly disappeared.

"Eric. What are you doing here?"

"Nice greeting," he said, stepping into the room. "I brought you some smashed-up flowers from the store. They're sort of ugly, but they still smell good."

"Thank you," she said, snatching the dilapidated bouquet from his hand. "Good-bye."

He closed the door and grabbed the flowers back. Two blossoms fell to the floor.

"I'll arrange them in a vase for you. You look very nice, by the way."

"Thank you. Eric, I am not a stupid person. You're here to check out Blake, and I want you to go home."

"Blake?" he repeated, heading for the kitchen. Nichelle was right behind him. "That's right. Tonight is your date with Pemberton. It slipped my mind."

"Ha! Go to the basketball game. Now!" A knock was again heard at the door. "Darn it, he's here. Eric, stay in this kitchen, do you hear me? Don't make a sound. Don't even breathe. I know you. You'll do your thug routine and I won't stand for it."

"Me?" he said, all innocence. "I just came over to bring you these flowers. I thought it was a rather nice gesture on my part."

She glared at him, then spun around and hurried to the door.

"Hello, Blake," she said. Again her smile slid off her chin as her gaze swept over him. Her heart began to race. The charcoal gray suit fit him to perfection. "Come in." The lighter gray shirt matched his eyes. His thick hair glowed like ebony. "How are you feeling?" He was beautiful, handsome beyond belief.

"I'm fine," he said. "Good as new. You look lovely, Nichelle." More than lovely, he thought. She was exquisite. "I must say I've been eager to see you without green hair." He'd been eager to see her, period. But her silken curls were beckoning him to weave his fingers through them.

"I'll get my purse and then we'll go."

"No rush. I made reservations, but we have plenty of time. You have a nice place here," he added, glancing around the room. It was decorated in pale yellow and mint green. "It looks like you—fresh, cheerful. Yes, I really like it."

"Thank you. We should go. The traffic will be heavy. And besides, this isn't a terrific neighborhood. You might get your hubcaps stolen."

"I have insurance."

"Well, yes, but think of the bother of filling out all those forms. We definitely should go."

Eric sneezed.

Blake stiffened.

Nichelle closed her eyes and fervently wished the floor would open up and swallow her.

"Is there someone in your kitchen?" Blake asked.

Nichelle opened her eyes and her mouth, but Eric appeared before she could speak.

"No-o-o," Eric said, slowly walking forward. "There's someone in her living room."

No joke, Blake thought. This guy was a mountain. Who in the hell was he, and what was he doing here?

"Aren't you going to introduce us, Nickie?" Eric asked.

"No. I mean, yes, of course. Blake Pemberton, this is Eric Franklin. Eric, this is Blake. Well, so much for that. Let's go, Blake."

"Eric?" Blake said. "You're the one who dyed Nichelle's hair green?"

"It was an accident," Nichelle said, all but wringing her hands. "My, my, I'm hungry. Shall we go to dinner, Blake?"

"I understand you live in Bel Air," Eric said, crossing his arms over his chest. He spread his legs slightly. Nichelle rolled her eyes.

"That's right," Blake said. He returned Eric's stare. A muscle jumped along his jaw, and Nichelle decided his eyes looked like cold chips of flint. "And I understand that you're Nichelle's neighbor."

"Yeah, I'm her neighbor, but more than that, I'm her friend. Kurt and I do our best to make sure that nothing happens to Nickie. We would be extremely upset if she were hurt in any way."

A heavy silence fell over the room as the two men studied each other, communicating in a language that Nichelle could not begin to fathom. She chewed nervously on the inside of her cheek as her eyes darted back and forth between the pair.

Blake suddenly relaxed and extended his hand to Eric. "Got it," he said, smiling.

Eric shook his hand. "You're pretty smart for an uptown dude. Enjoy your dinner."

"Ready, Nichelle?" Blake asked, turning to look at her.

"Huh? Oh, yes, of course." She snatched her purse up off the sofa. "Lock the door when you leave, Eric. 'Bye."

"Enjoy," Eric said pleasantly. Nichelle shot him a murderous look before she preceded Blake out of the apartment.

Outside, the air was crisp but felt heavenly on Nichelle's flushed face. The scene in her living room had jangled her nerves. Blake assisted her into his low-slung sports car, and was chuckling when he slid behind the wheel and turned the key in the ignition.

"That's quite a bodyguard you have there," he said as he pulled away from the curb.

"Eric means well. I'm sorry that happened, though."

"I'm not. This is a rough neighborhood, Nichelle, but I'm sure word has gotten out on the streets that you're well protected. That eases my mind. So does the fact that Eric and Kurt are more than just roommates sharing the rent."

"Who told you that?" she asked, her eyes widening.

"Eric did while we were standing in your living room."

"He did?"

"Yep, and I'm glad he and Kurt are there for you. I also know they'll wipe the floor with me if I hurt you. But, Nichelle, even if those guys weren't in the picture, I wouldn't do anything to hurt you. I hope you believe that. I realize you have . . . certain ideas about my lifestyle because of what you've seen in my apartment over the past several weeks. But I'm not a fool. I know you're different, special. I'd never take anything from you that you weren't willing to give."

Oh, how sweet, she thought.

"Do you trust me?" he asked, glancing over at her.

"Trust you?" she said, snapping out of her dreamy trance. She sighed. "No, I guess I don't. I realize that's a rotten thing to say, but I might as well be honest. Please don't misunderstand me, Blake. You apparently aren't standing in judgment of Eric and Kurt's lifestyle, and I'm not judging yours. I just know that I don't operate on the same plane as you do. I wouldn't know how to be a Miss Six-and-a-half-narrow if someone put a gun to my head."

"You don't sleep around," he said. It was a statement, not a question.

"No, I don't."

"I've already figured that out. Like I said, you're very special. And I'll also repeat that I'd never take anything from you that you weren't willing to give me."

"Blake . . ." She shifted on her seat to face him. "I think I should tell you that I don't intend to see you after tonight. You probably don't intend to see me again, anyway, but I prefer to get this out in the open. This date is a mistake."

"And the kiss we shared in my apartment? Was that a mistake too?"

Yes, her mind whispered, because she couldn't forget it. The memory of Blake's lips on hers was crystal-clear, as was the warm curl of desire within her that that memory evoked. "Yes. It was a mistake."

"No, Nichelle," he said, his voice low. "It wasn't. It was heaven itself and you know it. As for seeing each other again, let's just take this one step at a time." What? he asked himself. What in the hell was he doing? The plan had been firm. Feed her, take her home, forget her. Now he was keeping his foot in the door like a persistent salesman. He definitely had a screw loose. Not only was Nichelle the furthest thing possible from his type of woman, but she had a bodyguard that made Rambo look like a twit. He didn't need this hassle!

"Blake, look, I meant what I said. After tonight—"

"Nichelle," he interrupted, "let's put all that on hold for now, okay? Tell me about yourself. Is your family in Los Angeles?"

"No," she said quietly, "I have no family."

He glanced quickly at her. "None?"

"No."

"How long have you been alone?"

"Three years. But I'm really not alone. I have Eric and Kurt, and some other wonderful friends."

And him, Blake thought fiercely. He'd meant what he'd said. He'd never hurt Nichelle, never take simply for the sake of taking. He wanted to give, and he wanted to protect her. She wasn't going to dust him off after tonight. No, sir. Good Lord, listen to him. It was as though some stranger were taking over his brain.

And he had a sneaky suspicion it was a leprechaun.

Four

The restaurant that Blake had chosen was popular, and had spared no expense in creating an atmosphere that was romantic while catering to the tastes of the affluent. Blake and Nichelle were led to a small table covered by a white linen cloth and boasting water glasses of exquisitely thin crystal. Nichelle smiled weakly as a tuxedo-clad waiter handed them thick menus.

"Classy, huh?" Blake said as the waiter moved away. "It's not every guy who takes his lady to a restaurant that has penguins for waiters."

She looked at him in surprise, then laughed. "Is my lack of sophistication showing? I admit to being rather overwhelmed. This place is incredible, like something out of a movie."

"Would you rather go somewhere else?" he asked.

"Oh, no! It's fabulous. Just kick me under the table if I gawk too much."

His voice became unbearably intimate. "Nichelle, you're the most beautiful woman here." He held one of her hands, stroking her wrist with his thumb. "And I'd bet money that you're the most honest, open, down-to-earth woman in the room too. This place suits you, penguins and all. You deserve the finest there is."

She was mesmerized by his deep voice, by the rhythmic movements of his thumb, by the silver depths of his warm eyes. She couldn't move, could hardly breathe. As the room, and noise, and people disappeared into a hazy mist, she did feel beautiful and very special. She smiled with a happiness she couldn't suppress.

"Thank you," she said softly.

"No. I thank *you* for being here with me. Here comes another penguin to see if we want drinks. Would you like some wine?"

"Yes, that sounds very nice," she said, and slowly pulled her hand from his.

"The wine list, sir," the waiter said stiffly. "Would you care to order?"

"I dare say, old chap," Blake said in a terrible British accent. "It does seem like the proper thing to do and all that."

Nichelle dissolved in a fit of laughter. Blake winked at her. The waiter frowned.

The mood was set.

Their conversation was fast and light, the food delicious. Nichelle had to smother her laughter each time a waiter approached, for she now envisioned all of them as large, waddling penguins. She and Blake spoke of movies they'd seen, books they'd read, and the merits of various basketball teams. She was relaxed, enjoying Blake's interest in all that she said and basking in his warm gazes.

"Are you from Los Angeles originally?" he asked.

"No, I moved here three years ago from San Diego right after—after my mother died."

He frowned. "I'm sorry. And your father? You said you had no family. Has he been gone a long time?"

"Gone? Oh, yes, a very long time," she said, reaching for her water glass.

Damn, Blake thought, what a big mouth he had. He'd seen a flicker of pain in her dark eyes when he asked about her parents. She couldn't be more than twenty-two or three, although she looked even younger. She was too young to be alone. But she was doing all right, was the president of her own corporation. Nichelle Clay was quite a woman.

"I remember you telling me you started Leprechauns, Inc., two years ago," he said. "What did you do before that?"

Cried, she thought. "I worked as a waitress. Then got the idea for Leprechauns, Inc. I would hear the women complaining during their long, leisurely lunches that they couldn't find a good cleaning lady, or that they were tired of shopping for gifts for their husbands' employees at Christmas."

Thank goodness, her eyes were sparkling again, Blake thought. Obviously, the subject of her parents was taboo. "So you started a company that offered those services?" he asked.

"Yes. I put flyers out, tacked up notices on bulletin boards in grocery stores. Eric and Kurt snuck into the parking lot at the Dorothy Chandler pavilion when the L.A. Symphony was performing and put my ad under the windshield wipers of the ritzy cars. The calls started coming in. I did all the jobs myself at first, with Eric and Kurt helping out when they had time. Then I hired Marcella, and on it went."

"That's really great," Blake said. "Being in investments, I know how difficult it is for new companies to stay afloat. You should be very proud of yourself."

"I am," she said, laughing. "I mentally pat myself on the head all the time."

He smiled. "Good for you."

"I owe a great deal to Eric and Kurt. They encouraged me to take a chance and they helped so much. When I first came here I was . . . well, very unhappy, and they saw me through all that too. They're my family now."

"Is that why you haven't moved from that neighborhood?" Blake asked. "I mean," he added quickly, "your apartment is very nice, and you've fixed it up, but wouldn't you feel safer in a section of town that doesn't have such a high crime rate? I realize Eric and Kurt watch over you, but they can't be around every minute."

"Actually, Eric and Kurt are saving their money to buy a little house. But even if they move, I'll stay where I am. I'm comfortable there, in that neighborhood. I have no desire to attempt to be something I'm not. People who do that eventually pay the piper."

"I see," Blake said, but he really didn't. It was the natural order of things, he thought. You work hard, reap your success, and slowly change your standard of living to match the financial gain. There was something wrong here. Nichelle's voice had trembled when she'd spoken of not trying to be something she wasn't. What was she afraid of? What wasn't she telling him? He glanced up as their waiter approached the table.

"Would you care for dessert?" the waiter asked.

Blake looked questioningly at Nichelle.

"No, thank you," she said. "Just coffee, please."

"Two coffees," Blake said. And take your time, penguin, he added silently. He didn't want this evening to end yet. He didn't want to have to take Nichelle home and say good night. So much for the fastest dinner on record. But she was enchanting, absolutely lovely. And there were surprising depths beneath her sunny exterior. She was intelligent, independent, and yet he was aware of a vulnerability hidden behind the protective wall she had built around herself. A complicated woman was Nichelle Clay, and he definitely wanted a chance to figure out the puzzle—although he really didn't know why.

"Well, my goodness," he heard a woman say, "if it isn't Junior Pemberton."

His head snapped up and he groaned silently. He stood to greet the stout woman and her equally round husband standing beside their table.

"Hello, Mrs. Easterman," he said, forcing a smile. "Mr. Easterman."

"Hello, Junior," Mrs. Easterman said. "Oh, how handsome you look. I had lunch the other day with your mother and I was telling her what a handsome boy you are."

"Thank you. I'd like you to meet Nichelle Clay. Nichelle, this is Mr. and Mrs. Easterman."

"Hello," Nichelle said, smiling.

"Clay," Mrs. Esterman said musingly. "Oh, of course. I know your parents, dear. Esther and Jack are members of the country club. I remember Esther saying their daughter was on an extended tour of Europe. Did you have a marvelous trip?"

"Oh, I'm not—" Nichelle started.

"Yes, marvelous," Blake interrupted. "She's been telling me all about it."

"Come along, Mother," Mr. Easterman said. "Let's leave these young people alone."

"Certainly," Mrs. Easterman cooed. "Oh, you are both so attractive. What a splendid couple you make. Will we see you at the country club dance next week?"

"You bet," Blake said. "Good night."

"Good night," Mrs. Easterman said, and bustled away with Mr. Easterman plodding along behind her.

Blake settled back into his chair, then the waiter appeared with their coffee. Nichelle watched as Blake casually stirred a spoonful of sugar into his cup.

"Why did you do that?" she asked, her voice strained.

"I always take sugar in my coffee," he said, confused.

"That isn't what I mean. Why did you let those people believe I was from your country-club crowd?"

He shrugged. "It was easier that way."

She rested her arms on the table and leaned toward him.

"Easier than what?" she asked angrily. "Explaining that Junior Pemberton was out with the hired help? Easier than explaining that the extent of my traveling consists of moving here from San Diego?"

"Hey, now, wait a minute," he said, raising his hand. "All I was trying to do was get rid of them. Mrs. Easterman is a busybody and would have stood here for an hour quizzing you."

"So? Would it have embarrassed you to have it known that you were out with your cleaning lady?"

"Dammit, Nichelle, knock it off. I don't like nosy women, okay? It's no one's business but mine who I go out with. I let her believe what she wanted so she'd get the hell out of here. Don't insinuate that I wouldn't want it known who you really are, what you do for a living. You're the president of your own corporation, for cripe's sake. Personally, I wouldn't care if you *were* just a cleaning lady. What difference does it make? Give me a little credit here. You're beginning to sound like someone with a very big chip on her shoulder."

She sat back in her chair, her arms crossed as she stared at Blake. Nice spiel, she thought, but it didn't erase the fact that he had passed her off as a globe-trotting debutante. Unless . . . he really had been trying to send Mrs. Easterman on her way. No, a simple statement would have set the record straight. But then again . . . Oh, darn it, she was getting terribly confused. Going out with Blake had been a mistake. She didn't belong here. She didn't.

"Come on, Nichelle," he said gently. "I apologize if I insulted you in some way. That certainly wasn't my intention. If I see anyone else I know, I'll announce in capital letters that you're a leprechaun, who has been known to have green hair on occasion. Okay?"

She sighed and relaxed her stiff posture. "I'm sorry," she said quietly. "I guess I do sound as though I have a chip on my shoulder. It's not that exactly. It's just that I have a very clear picture of who I am and where I belong."

"People aren't assigned slots, Nichelle. We change, grow, take on new things when the time is right. You said that Eric and Kurt are saving for a house. That's an example of working hard, then reaping the rewards of the labor. I get the feeling you don't think any of that natural order of progress applies to you."

"I already have everything I need. I've bought the furniture and nice clothes I used to fantasize about. I have money in the bank and a fairly secure future. To look further would be foolish and dangerous."

"Why? We never stop growing, reaching for new dreams. That's healthy, not dangerous. Why don't you want more? What about a husband, children, a home? Where is it etched in stone that you're to live alone in a high-crime neighborhood for the rest of your life? What are you afraid of?"

"Stop it," she said, staring into her coffee. "You don't understand."

"Then explain it to me," he said, again taking her hand. "I want to understand you. Talk to me, Nichelle."

"No," she said, shaking her head. "I'd like to go home, Blake."

He stared at her for a long moment, then with a tight set to his jaw signaled to the waiter.

"I'll wait for you by the door," she said.

He watched her cross the room, seeing the determined tilt to her chin, the stiff set to her shoulders and back.

Dammit, he fumed, tossing a credit card onto the silver plate the waiter produced. The entire evening was shot to hell. Nichelle was shutting him out, retreating further behind her walls, and he didn't know why. She was frightened of something and obviously didn't trust him. Well, he had news for that leprechaun. He wasn't being dusted off!

When he joined her at the door he smiled at her. She did not smile back. He helped her into his car and neither spoke as he pulled out onto the road.

Nichelle stared out the side window. She was exhausted.

She was also, she told herself, a lousy Cinderella. She didn't even get to be what she wasn't until midnight. She'd come down off her rosy cloud with a thud. She just wanted to go home, crawl into bed, and sleep. She shouldn't have gone out with Blake. Eric had tried to warn her, but she'd been so sure she could handle a few stolen hours. She'd overreacted to the way Blake had dealt with the Eastermans, and had hurled unfair accusations at him. He was probably very relieved the evening was about to end.

"Nichelle?" he said finally.

"Yes?"

"We're not ending it like this. You know that, don't you?"

"Ending?" she repeated, turning to look at him. "Nothing began."

"Wrong. Something began the moment you beamed yourself down into my bedroom as a green-haired alien. And that something grew when we kissed in my kitchen."

"No."

"Yes." He glanced at her. "You can sit there and deny it, but we both know it's true. You're determined not to give us a chance to discover what all this means. I don't think it's fair that you're calling the shots on something that involves both of us. I don't like being told what to do, Nichelle."

"I'm not telling—"

"And another thing," he went on, ignoring her retort. "I don't appreciate being labeled. You seem to have pegged me as a hustler because of things you've seen in my apartment over the past three months. You're also a social snob."

"What!" she shrieked.

Oh, Pemberton, he thought, you are probably a breath away from being dead meat. "You heard me. You've drawn a mental line down this city and anyone on the other side from you doesn't measure up. Am I supposed to apologize for living in Bel Air, for working my buns off to get what I have? Who in the hell do you think you are, passing judgment on me?" This was either brilliant or the dumbest thing he'd ever done, he thought. But, hell, he was desperate. He had to try *something*. Did Nichelle pack enough of a wallop to break his nose?

Nichelle could feel her fury building inside her. She drew a deep breath and said the first thing that came to her mind.

"Fie on you, Blake Pemberton!"

"What?" He stared blankly at her. "Fie on you? Oh, good Lord." He burst into laughter. "I can't believe you actually said that. What have you got against a good old 'go to hell' or 'take a flying leap'? Fie on you? Oh, that's rich. I love it."

"I read it in a book once," she said, and a bubble of laughter escaped from her own lips. "I'm counting on fie being something absolutely grim."

Blake was still laughing as he pulled into the parking lot of her apartment building. She smiled in spite of herself as he opened her door, but felt her gloomy mood return as they stepped out of the elevator and walked down the corridor to her door.

"Are your bodyguards around?" Blake whispered.

"No, Eric and Kurt are out," she said, reaching into her purse for her key.

He took the key from her and opened the door, then stepped back for her to enter. She flicked the wall switch to bring the lamps on the end tables alive. When she turned back to Blake, he was leaning against the doorjamb.

Tell him good night, she instructed herself. Tell him good-bye. She had to close the door. "Would you like a brandy?" she asked.

"Sure," Blake said, pushing away from the doorjamb. He closed the door and pulled the knot of his tie down a couple of inches. "Do you mind if I take off my jacket?"

"Go right ahead. I'll get the drinks." Why on earth was she doing this? she asked herself as she went into the kitchen. Postponing Blake's leaving wasn't going to change the ultimate outcome. He'd go out of that door, and that would be that. If he felt she was telling him what to do, that was just too bad. She had to do what she had to do.

When she returned to the living room, Blake was sitting on the sofa. After handing him a brandy snifter, she sat down a full cushion away from him. She sipped her brandy, then set the glass on the coffee table. She could feel Blake's gaze on her, and turned her head slowly to look at him. Their eyes met, held, and she felt her heart begin to beat wildly.

He was so magnificent, she thought. Magnificent to touch, to feel, to taste.

Looking directly into her eyes, he set his own glass on the coffee table and moved closer to her.

"I told you," he said, his voice low, "that I'd ask your permission to kiss you good night. So, I'm asking. May I kiss you, Nichelle?"

No! her mind screamed.

Yes, her heart whispered.

"Yes."

He wove his fingers into her hair and leaned slowly toward her. She could feel his warm breath on her skin as his gaze swept over her face, feature by feature, before coming to rest on her slightly parted lips.

"You are so beautiful," he murmured, then covered her mouth with his.

It was ecstasy. Nichelle splayed her hands on Blake's back, relishing the feel of his hard, strong body, and he slid his own arms around her, bringing her closer, crushing her breasts against his chest. His tongue plunged into her mouth, and desire flared deep within her as they drank of each other.

Blake lifted his head only long enough to draw air into his lungs, then captured Nichelle's mouth once more; wanting, needing, taking, giving. *Ah, Nichelle.*

Nichelle savored the sensations rocketing through her, igniting a heated path of desire as they tumbled within her. It was a shattering pleasure, a sensual promise of what this man could bring to her. *Oh, Blake.*

Blake explored every hidden crevice of her mouth, his tongue teasing, coaxing, arousing her passion to a fever pitch. She moaned softly, and the sound caused a shudder to rip through him. His hands moved to the waistband of her sweater, then beneath it to rest on the soft skin of her back. He inched upward, and she drew away to give him access to her breasts. His lips drifted over her face as his palms cupped her breasts, his thumbs stroking the nipples to taut buttons through her lacy bra.

"Nichelle," he murmured, and sought her lips once more.

His voice was a caress, and she felt as though she

were floating on a glorious cloud. She gripped Blake's shoulders for support as she welcomed the demands of his lips and tongue. Her body hummed with desire. She pressed more tightly to him, delighting in the sweet torture of his hands stroking her aching breasts. Heat churned within her, pulsing with a message of need.

Dear heaven, how she wanted this man.

He pulled his legs onto the sofa and leaned back, taking her with him. She lay along his muscled length, his manhood pressing hard against her. She shifted her hips ever so slightly and he groaned deep in his chest.

Then he went completely still.

Perplexed, she lifted her head to meet his gaze. His eyes were smoky with desire and beads of sweat shone on his forehead. He slowly withdrew his hands from beneath her sweater and gripped her upper arms.

"I want you," he said, his voice rough with passion. "I want you so damn much. I have to stop, Nichelle. I have to before it's too late."

"But I . . ."

"I told you I'd never hurt you, never take anything from you that you weren't ready to give me. I meant it. You want me, Nichelle. Every beautiful, wonderful inch of you is telling me that you do, but I'm not sure that you're thinking clearly. When we make love, it will be a mutual decision with no regrets. This isn't the night."

He lifted her up and away from him, seemingly with no effort, and swung his feet to the floor. She blinked once slowly as a wave of dizziness washed over her. In rather detached fascination she watched

Blake meticulously straighten her sweater, his hands trembling slightly as he concentrated on smoothing it, as if this were of the utmost importance.

Somewhere in the far recesses of her mind she realized that he was using the time to gain control of his raging passion, and she smiled crookedly. Finally he moved away, turning to face her, and he took her hands in his as he looked directly into her eyes.

"I'm leaving now, Nichelle," he said, "but I'll be back. We owe it to ourselves to find out what this is that's happening between us. I want you, but it's more than that. Good night, leprechaun."

He brushed his lips over hers and stood up.

Nichelle didn't move, didn't speak. She was vaguely aware of him pulling on his jacket, crossing the room. The quiet click of the door as he closed it behind him seemed to be magnified tenfold, and she jerked in surprise.

"Oh, good heavens," she said, her hands flying to her flushed cheeks. "Oh, good grief. Oh, my. What have I done?"

Nothing major, she rationalized. She'd simply adhered herself to Blake Pemberton's body and responded to his kisses, his touches with total abandon. She'd only felt mind-boggling and wondrous sensations that she'd never felt before. She'd wanted to tear off their clothes and make love with him until she was too weak to move. That's all she'd done. No big deal.

"Oh, good Lord." She shook her head. "I can't believe I did that."

She reached for her snifter and took a deep swallow. "Aaagh," she gasped, clutching her neck as the fiery brandy burned her throat.

Why? she asked herself, staring into the amber liquid. Why Blake? Why was he capable of running roughshod over her senses? Why did she desire him with such intensity and miss him the moment he walked out the door?

She took another drink of the brandy, but when tears sprang to her eyes from the powerful liquor she decided enough was enough. She set the snifter back on the coffee table with the fervent hope that she hadn't dissolved her tonsils. She pulled her knees up, wrapped her arms around her legs, and rested her chin on her knees.

Memories of Blake's kisses, the feel of his hands on her breasts, crept in around her, accompanied by whispers of sensual heat. Oh, she was acting so ditzy, she fumed. She wasn't a blushing innocent, for crying out loud. She was a sexually experienced woman of the eighties.

What a crock, she admitted an instant later. She'd had one disastrous, brief affair during her I-am-woman-because-I'm-twenty-one number. No, she wasn't worldly and wise. The men she dated were friendly, fun, and nothing more. She kissed them good night at the door and that was that. What Blake stirred in her was new. Startling. Wonderful. And scary as hell. Because, oh, darn, he was the wrong man!

But how was she going to erase Blake from her mind? How could she ever forget the feel of him, the taste of him, the marvelous things he did to her body, just by talking in that low, sexy voice of his?

She sighed. It was a sad sigh that spoke of her inner turmoil and confusion. Wearily she locked the door and turned off the lights, then got ready for bed.

Clad in a flannel nightgown with a pattern of playful kittens on it, she crawled into bed. With the blankets pulled up to her chin she stared into the darkness. The image of Blake danced before her eyes and, without thinking, she pressed her fingers to her lips. Her breasts seemed to swell and the now-familiar desire churned deep within her.

"Oh, fie on you, Blake Pemberton," she said, and flopped over onto her stomach.

But it was hours later before she finally fell into an uneasy slumber.

At two A.M. Blake threw back his blankets and strode naked into the living room. He couldn't sleep. He'd totally demolished the sheets with his restless tossing and had finally given up the battle. The image of Nichelle Clay had followed him home, taunted him during his icy cold shower, then scrambled right into bed with him.

She was driving him crazy!

He had to think this through, he decided as he paced the room. He was becoming obsessed with Nichelle, and he wasn't sure why. Why was he messing around with a woman who passed judgment on his lifestyle and the size of his bank account? Why was he putting himself through sexual frustration when he knew plenty of women who were willing to accommodate him?

He could have had her right there on her sofa, he thought. His great display of nobility had been ridiculous. She'd wanted him. There'd been no doubt about it. All he'd gotten out of the deal was an ache in his gut and a cold shower that had proven to be worthless.

Well, that wasn't quite true, he admitted. He'd had Nichelle in his arms. He'd touched and kissed her, been surrounded by her softness, her sweet aroma, gloried in the fact that she responded to him, had wanted him. When he'd stopped their love-making, he had known it was the right thing to do. He wouldn't make love to her until she was very sure that was what she wanted. He would never hurt her. She was special, rare.

And not his type. That was the bottom line. He needed a plan to get Nichelle out of his head. She was different from the women he knew and, therefore, was fascinating. Check. Once he figured her out, the fascination would dim and he'd regain control of his mind and body. Check. All he had to do was see as much of Nichelle as possible as quickly as possible, figure out what made her tick, then fade into the sunset. Check. Lord, he was brilliant.

"Fie on you, Nichelle Clay," he said, and strode back into the bedroom.

Despite the rumpled state of the bedcovers he fell asleep within minutes. His last conscious thought, accompanied by a smug smile, was that everything was under control. Check.

Five

Every Saturday morning Nichelle rode the bus to the Pueblo, the Mexican village in the heart of Los Angeles, to shop for fresh fruit and vegetables. Open stalls lined Olvera Street, offering colorful merchandise in addition to the produce. Musicians playing Mexican music wandered through the crowds, lending a festive air.

In spite of Nichelle's near-sleepless night, she still eagerly anticipated her visit to the noisy, crowded, colorful marketplace. Dressed in jeans and a fluffy pink sweater, she picked up her purse and two handwoven straw shopping bags, and left the apartment. She was humming a cheerful tune as she stepped out of the elevator and crossed the lobby to the front doors of the building.

As she pushed open the door on the right, Blake Pemberton tugged on the one on the left.

"Blake," she gasped. "What are you doing here?"

Her gaze swept over him. In tight jeans, with a white shirt beneath a red V-neck sweater, he was beautiful. Absolutely beautiful.

"Hi," he said, smiling broadly. What she did for jeans and a sweater should be illegal, he thought. And those bouncy, silky curls were just begging to be touched. She was so lovely.

They stood there for a timeless moment, leaning against the doors as they gazed into each other's eyes. Nichelle wondered if Blake could hear the wild thudding of her heart. Blake felt as though he'd sprinted five miles and there was no air left in his lungs.

"You people attached to them doors or what?" a man asked.

Nichelle tore her gaze from Blake and glanced at the man standing behind her. She smiled rather dreamily at him.

"Door?" she murmured, her voice breathless. She blinked. "Oh! This door. Yes. Well. Sure thing. I'm going out of it right now. 'Bye."

She stepped back, holding the door open for the man, who grumbled his way through with the ugliest bulldog Nichelle had ever seen.

"Cute dog," she said.

She released the door at the same time that Blake let go of his, and they met in the middle of the walkway.

"Hi," he said again, smiling down at her.

"Why are you here?" she asked. To kiss her? she wondered. Oh, she hoped so. Just one kiss, that was all. Just one delicious kiss.

"I'm here . . ." To kiss her, he thought. Lord, he wanted to haul her into his arms and kiss the living daylights out of her. ". . . To . . ." He cleared his throat. ". . . See you. You know, just drop by and say hello, ask what's doin', that sort of thing. So! Nichelle! What's doin'?"

She eyed him suspiciously. "I'm going shopping for fruit and vegetables."

"Great," he said, taking her arm. "I'll go with you."

Nichelle didn't move. "You want to go shopping for fruit and vegetables? You, the gourmet of beer and frozen dinners, are going to the market?"

"I'm broadening my horizons, expanding my knowledge of the mundane. It'll be a peak experience. Let's go."

"Wait a minute. I doubt seriously that you want to go where I'm going. It's not your type of area. The Pueblo is far removed from Bel Air, Blake, in more than just miles."

He narrowed his eyes. "Are you doing your social-snob routine again?"

"All I'm saying is that—"

"Coming through," someone yelled. "Delivery to make. Move it or lose it."

"Oh, for Pete's sake," Nichelle muttered, and spun around and marched away.

Blake stepped back to make room for a teenager carrying a large box.

"Get the door, mister?" the boy asked.

"Yeah, sure," Blake said. He opened the door, willed the youth to get the lead out, then hurried after Nichelle, who was walking down the sidewalk. "Hey, wait up!" He fell in step beside her.

"I'm not a social snob," she said, sticking her nose in the air. "That's a very demeaning thing to say."

"We'll put that on the back burner for now. Where

is your car parked? Don't you use the lot at your building?"

"I don't own a car."

"Hold it." He placed his hand flat on the top of her head to halt her flight.

She stopped and glared up at him. "You're smushing my hair. Can't you walk and talk at the same time?"

"My dear," he said, dropping his hand and grinning at her, "you would be awed by all the things I can do at the same time."

"Spare me the details."

"If you insist. Let's back up here. Why don't you own a car?"

She shrugged. "I don't know how to drive. Besides, I can get everywhere I need to go on the bus."

"You go all the way to Bel Air every Wednesday morning on the bus? You're going shopping for fruit and vegetables on the bus?"

"My dear," she said, leaning toward him and wiggling her eyebrows, "you would be awed by all the things I can do on a bus."

"Not funny," he said, scowling. "Come on. We're going in my car."

"Okey-dokey," she said breezily. "I just hope you're not sentimentally attached to your hubcaps."

"We've covered that ground already. I have insurance, remember?"

They turned and started back toward her apartment building. The morning air was miraculously free of smog and she tilted her head back to allow the warm sun to wash over her face. She suddenly felt lighthearted and happy, young and carefree.

And she knew why.

Blake was with her.

Be it wrong or be it right, Blake was with her in all his male splendor—tall, and dark, and strong, and, oh, so enticing. He was filling her senses with his very essence. She didn't want to think, not today. She just wanted to enjoy the sunshine, the sound of the birds singing in the trees, and Blake.

Her whimsical thoughts came back to earth with a thud. Blake Pemberton in the Pueblo? she wondered. His sweater probably cost more than some of those people made in a week. The Pueblo was earthy and real, and a world away from Bel Air. He'd hate it. She loved it. So be it. Blake would see for himself that their lives didn't mesh, that there actually was an invisible line separating them. Neither of them would be truly comfortable crossing over that line. She wasn't a social snob, she was a realist. Facts were facts.

As they drove out of the parking lot she gave Blake directions to the Pueblo.

"Got it," he said, nodding. "You really don't know how to drive?"

"Nope. We never owned a car."

"I could teach you."

"Thank you for the offer, but I do just fine on the bus."

"There are weirdos on buses, Nichelle. You'd be a lot safer in your own car."

"There are weirdos on the freeways too, bub. I'll stick with my buses."

"You should give this more thought," he said, glancing over at her. "I'm sure you could get a bank to finance a car. After all, you're the president of your own corporation."

"Oh, I have enough money saved to buy a car, but I have no intention of spending my nest egg. It's my security for the future."

"That's important to you, isn't it? That sense of security."

"Very important," she said seriously. "But it's not just money, Blake. It's knowing where I belong, knowing that what I have is mine, and no one can take it away from me because I've earned it by honest labor. I never have to be afraid that when I open the door there will be a bill collector demanding . . ." Her voice trailed off and she looked out her window. "Never mind."

"Demanding money?" he prodded gently.

She nodded, then stared down at her hands.

"Then we'd move again," she said, her voice trembling. "We'd sneak off in the middle of the night, me and my mother, like thieves. We could never stay, not for long. I loved my mother, I truly did. But, oh, God, I hated that life. If only she hadn't—I don't want to talk about this anymore."

Blake turned onto a side street and parked under a large tree. Nichelle looked at him questioningly and his heart slammed against his ribs when he saw the tears misting her big dark eyes. He cradled her face in his hands.

"Nichelle."

He said her name with a tenderness and warmth that was reflected on his face, and a sob caught in her throat. Then he kissed her. A soft, gentle kiss. A kiss-to-make-it-better kiss that caused two tears to slide down her cheeks.

"You don't have to be afraid of anything," he said, his lips close to hers. "Not ever again."

He kissed her once more and she wrapped her arms around his neck, opening to him. She chased her distressing thoughts to a dusty corner of her mind, and returned Blake's kiss with a sweet, aching yearning for more. The heat of his solid body wove into her, chasing away the chill her bleak memories had brought to her soul. Desire swirled within her and she relished each tantalizing sensation that swept through her. It was heaven.

Blake shifted his hands to her back to pull her closer, closer, as his mouth ravished hers. Blood pounded in his veins. The needs of his body intertwined with those of his heart, tumbling together in a jumbled mix.

The sight of Nichelle's tears had been like a knife twisting in his gut, and a cold fury had raged through him. He was slowly piecing together a picture of what Nichelle's life had been like and he hated what he saw. Somehow he knew he was fighting against ghosts from her past, and he wanted to beat them into submission.

Blake lifted his mouth from hers and nestled her head against his shoulder. His fingers wove through her hair as he strove for control. His breathing was rough and labored, and he made no attempt to speak. He simply held her. She felt so fragile, so small in his arms, and he had the irrational thought that if he kept her in his embrace, his strength would pass from him to her.

At that moment, sitting in a car beneath a magnificent old tree that had withstood the rigors of time, Blake Pemberton knew he was falling in love with Nichelle Clay.

He was filled with immeasurable joy. A smile formed

on his lips and he buried his face in her fragrant hair. His heart raced, and his throat tightened with emotion. He had found what he hadn't even known he was seeking—Nichelle, his leprechaun, his love.

She stirred in his arms and he reluctantly released her, only then realizing the gear shift was jammed against his thigh. She slowly opened her eyes and he stared at her as if he were seeing her for the first time.

"Hi," he said, trailing his thumb over her cheek.

"I'm sorry," she said. "I don't know what happened. Everything just came rushing back at me and . . . I'm very sorry."

"Please don't say that, Nichelle. You were sharing yourself with me, and that's so very important. I know you don't want to discuss it anymore now, but another time, when you're ready, you should tell me the rest, fill in the missing pieces."

"No," she said, shaking her head. "It has nothing to do with my life today."

"I think maybe it does."

"No."

"Okay, we'll drop it for now. Do you want to go home? You look all worn out."

"No, I really need to do my shopping."

"Your wish is my command," he said, smiling. And her sorrow and pain were his, he thought, her smile his sunshine, her laughter his song. Dear heaven, how he loved her. "Nichelle . . ."

"Yes?"

"I'm in the mood for a great big juicy peach. Think you can pick me out a beauty?"

She smiled. "Absolutely."

"Then let's go." He turned the key in the ignition, but she placed her hand on his arm.

"Blake?"

"Yes?"

"Thank you."

Their eyes met and messages of greater understanding and awareness were silently exchanged. It was a quiet moment, a special moment, then Nichelle turned away and Blake pulled back onto the street.

Why? Nichelle wondered. Why had the past come rushing back with its painful, haunting memories? It had been two years since she'd cried for her mother, and for herself.

She glanced at Blake, and she knew why she'd remembered that awful time. It was Blake, all that he was, and all that she couldn't have.

But she didn't want to let him go!

She must, she told herself. She wouldn't follow the path of heartbreak that her mother had chosen. Blake Pemberton was not hers to have.

She looked at him again and resisted the urge to touch him, to feel his warmth and strength. She was so alive when he held her. She felt beautiful and more like a woman than she'd ever felt before.

Dear heaven, she thought, was she falling in love with this man? Oh, no, she mustn't do that. But how did she stop it from happening? What should she do?

She sighed and Blake immediately looked at her.

"What's wrong?" he asked.

"Nothing," she said, forcing a smile. "I was just thinking. We're almost to the Pueblo. I'm not sure what the parking situation is. I've never paid any attention."

"One of the perks of riding the bus, huh? You don't have to worry about finding a place to park."

"Or having my hubcaps stolen."

He chuckled, then turned onto a side street. There was a parking space there that seemed to have been waiting just for him. As they walked toward the main area of the Pueblo, the buzz of voices and sound of music became increasingly louder, and Nichelle grew increasingly tense. What would Blake think of all this? she wondered. Would he see the vibrant colors as gaudy, the boisterous people as rough and uncouth? Would the rich aromas of Mexican food that made her mouth water seem to him greasy odors that hung heavily in the air? She peeked at him from beneath her lashes. He was looking around, no readable expression on his face.

Darn it, she thought with an unexpected flash of anger, what was she getting uptight about? She wasn't apologizing for a place she adored; not for the people, the sights, the sounds, or the smells. She wasn't trying to impress Blake Pemberton from Bel Air. If he didn't like it here, it was too darn bad. He had invited himself along on this junket, and he could keep his complaints to himself. One word, just one derogatory word from him and she'd tell him where he could put himself and his zillion-dollar sweater.

"Nichelle?"

"What?" she said crossly.

"We're still going to be here at lunchtime, aren't we? I love homemade Mexican food. My taste buds are going nuts."

Her eyes widened. "I beg your pardon? You want to eat lunch here?"

He inhaled deeply. "Can't you smell that? Tacos, flour tortillas, tamales. I'm going to have a feast. Okay." He rubbed his hands together. "Where do we start? Fruits and veggies, right? Let's get the boring junk out of the way so we can look at the good stuff. Why is your mouth open?"

She snapped her mouth closed, spun around, and marched in the direction of the fruit stand she frequented. The good stuff? she repeated to herself. Blake wanted to stroll through the Pueblo and see what was available at the other booths? They were going to eat lunch here? His gray eyes were sparkling like those of a little boy who had just been turned loose in a candy store.

Well, damn, she thought, this wasn't going right at all. He was supposed to turn his snooty Bel Air nose up at the Pueblo, not be raring to go, eager to see every inch of it. He was grinning from ear to ear, for Pete's sake. And she wanted to plant kisses over his entire gorgeous face. Blake Pemberton was definitely full of surprises.

"Nickie," the woman behind the fruit stand called as they approached. "Hello."

"Hello, Olivia," Nichelle said, smiling. "How are you?"

"Fine, fine. I have luscious fruit for you today. Oh, and I set aside a special cantaloupe for Eric and Kurt. They love cantaloupe."

"I know. They squabble over who gets the biggest piece. Olivia, this is Blake Pemberton. Blake, this is Olivia Ortega. Her daughter, Marcella, is a leprechaun."

"Oh, I see," Blake said, extending his hand to Olivia. "It's a pleasure meeting you, Mrs. Ortega."

"Call me Olivia. We're all family in the Pueblo. Nickie is like a daughter to me. And Eric and Kurt are like sons. Those two, God bless them, painted my little house for me last year as my birthday present. I cried happy tears for three days. My Marcella is going to UCLA, thanks to Nickie arranging Marcella's leprechaun schedule around her classes. Oh, this Nickie, she brings such joy to our lives."

And she was going to bring it all to his life, too, Blake thought, feeling smug and possessive. When he fell in love, he didn't mess around. His Nichelle was really something.

"Now we choose fruit," Olivia said, planting her hands on her ample hips. She looked directly at Blake. "We want only the best for our Nickie. We wouldn't rest easy if Nickie didn't have what she deserved."

"Got it," he said, nodding slowly. Holy smoke, he thought incredulously, he'd just been threatened by the Mexican Mafia or something. Nichelle was family and they took care of their own. It was nice. He could end up with broken kneecaps, but it was still nice. He'd never been a part of anything like this. "Don't worry about a thing, Olivia."

She continued to study him and he met her gaze steadily. Nichelle was busy looking over the plums.

"*Bueno,*" Olivia finally said, smiling broadly. "*Sí, muy bueno.* Welcome to the Pueblo, Blake Pemberton."

"Thank you," he said, and released a rush of air. He hadn't realized he'd been holding his breath.

"Blake wants a big, juicy peach," Nichelle said.

"Then you choose it for him, Nickie," Olivia said. "Take your time, don't rush. You'll know what is right for you to give to Blake."

Olivia wasn't talking about peaches, Nichelle thought as a flush heated her cheeks. It was as though Olivia were peering into her mind, her heart, and could see her growing feelings for Blake. He had, apparently, passed Olivia's approval and now Olivia was telling her to listen to her inner voice. But it was all so much more complicated than that. Had Blake picked up on the underlying message in Olivia's words?

"I'll wait," he said quietly to her. "Take all the time you need . . . selecting my peach."

Her head snapped up and she saw the warmth and tenderness in his eyes, the gentle smile on his lips. Her heart thudded against her ribs as she realized he hadn't missed a single nuance in Olivia's veiled statements. She was torn between wanting to run away as fast as her feet would carry her and throwing herself into Blake's arms. Fearing her thoughts were reflected in her eyes, she turned back to stare at the plums.

As she filled one of her straw bags with fruit, she forced herself to relax. She chose a huge peach for Blake, which he consumed with obvious pleasure. Olivia stored the bag beneath the stand, and when Nichelle returned with the other bag full of vegetables, she tucked it under there too.

"Now, go, shoo," Olivia said, flapping her hands at them. "Have fun. Every booth is open today. There're lots of treasures to explore."

"We're off," Blake said. He circled Nichelle's shoulders with his arm and led her away. "Hey, look at those chili bowls. Too bad I don't know how to make chili. Maybe I'll buy my mother some chili bowls. What do you think, Nichelle?"

What did she think? She thought that Blake was stealing into her heart and staking a claim on it, inch by emotional inch. She was teetering on the edge of falling in love, and she was exhilarated and frightened in the same breathless moment.

"Nichelle?"

"What? Oh, I think the bowls are very nice. Does your mother make chili?"

"You bet. My dad polishes off three bowls without coming up for air."

"You've never mentioned your father before," she said as she picked up one of the bowls.

"He's the finest man I know. I love him, I like him, I respect him. My mother is a little scatterbrained, but my dad worships her. They're beautiful together."

"That's lovely."

Blake chuckled. "On the day I graduated from college my dad gave my bed to a secondhand store. He had it hauled right out the front door."

"Why?"

"He said he'd paid for my education and now the rest was up to me. I was a man, and it was time for me to stand on my own two feet. There were four other bedrooms in that house, but I got the message. He moved the bed of my youth out to make his point."

"How did you feel about it?"

"Determined. Very, very determined. I got a job and my own apartment—which was wonderful, by the way. It contained a card table, a lamp, and the best damn bed money could buy. Lord, I was proud of that bed. I worked hard, learned the investment business, then started my own company five years ago. I owe a helluva lot to that foxy old coot who gave my bed away. The story of my life. Enough. I want some chili bowls!"

She blinked away the tears that had misted her eyes as he began to examine the pottery bowls. Blake had worked for everything he had, she realized. Granted, he'd had the benefit of an education, but he'd done the rest himself. She understood how much love it had taken for his father to give away that bed. But more important, Blake understood it. The Pembertons knew how to love.

A few minutes later Nichelle laughed in delight as she watched the animated exchange between Blake and the pottery vendor. Blake was studying each bowl as though he were about to purchase an expensive gem. The vendor loudly declared the merits of each, while Blake said noncommittally, "Mmm." He finally selected six bowls.

"Fantastic," he said to Nichelle after the vendor had handed him his purchase. "I'm telling you, Nichelle, these are state-of-the-art chili bowls."

She smiled and slipped her arm through his, and they wandered on to the next booth, then to the ones after that. Lunch was a delicious combination of tacos, freshly made flour tortillas with refried beans, and tall glasses of iced tea. They ate at a paint-stained picnic table with a man and woman and their four children. Blake winked at the little girl, who was about six, and she dissolved in a giggling fit. Blake hooted with laughter. Nichelle smiled at him and felt a warm inner glow from her nose to her toes.

It was a wonderful day, Nichelle thought. It was sunshine and fresh air, laughter and lighthearted fun. Blake pulled her close at every opportunity, and brushed kisses over her temple. They shared smiles, and there were timeless moments when they simply stared into each other's eyes. They sat on a brick wall and listened to music, and she groaned when Blake said he was ready for more tacos. The first streaks of the California sunset were drifting across the sky when she announced that she was exhausted.

"So soon?" he asked in mock amazement. "Where's your vim? Where's your vigor?"

"You dimmed my vim when you insisted we take part in the Mexican hat dance."

"How'd you like my fancy footwork?"

"It was great until you stepped on the hat."

"That guy sure got hot when I smashed his hat. I bought him two new ones though. He didn't have to threaten to make taco meat out of me. I wonder if he decided to steal my hubcaps."

"I hope not," she said, smiling. "Let's go collect my goodies from Olivia."

"Okay. Hey, wait a minute. I didn't see that booth over there before."

"You didn't miss any of them, Blake. My feet are positive of that."

He grabbed her hand. "Come on. I have to check this out." She rolled her eyes, then scrambled to keep up with his long-legged stride.

He stopped in front of the booth, set the sack containing his chili bowls on the ground, and wiped his hands on his jeans before reaching for the white shawl hanging from one of the roof supports. It was delicately woven. Made of baby-fine wool, it reminded Nichelle of an airy cloud.

"Would you look at this?" Blake asked, holding it

up carefully. "Did you make it?" he asked the young woman behind the counter.

She nodded. "*Sí*."

"Isn't this something, Nichelle?"

"Yes, it's really lovely."

He turned to her and draped it around her shoulders. He pulled it gently forward, his hands brushing across her breasts. Nichelle's breath quickened.

"Beautiful," he said, looking directly into her eyes. "You're so beautiful. I want to buy this for you, Nichelle."

"No—"

"Please," he interrupted. "It will be a memento from today. A wonderful day. Our day." The day he'd discovered he loved her, he thought. He wanted to tell her how he felt, but he knew she wasn't ready to hear the words yet. She was skittish, his little leprechaun, so he'd wait. "Okay? Will you accept the shawl?"

"I . . . yes, all right. Thank you, Blake. And thank you for today."

He kissed her on the forehead, then slowly withdrew the shawl from her shoulders. The young woman wrapped it in white tissue paper and handed it to Nichelle.

"I must put it in the hands of the one who will wear it," she said. "You must follow the tradition of the white shawl."

"Tradition?" Nichelle repeated.

"You must wear it only for your lover, the man you love, no one but him. Then you must remember to hold it to your breast for a moment on your wedding day."

"Oh, well . . . um . . ." Her face turned crimson.

"Go on," Blake said to the woman. "What else?"

"Your firstborn baby will be wrapped in the shawl on his christening day. Then it must be put away until the day of death so you will be wearing it when you meet your lover again in a greater place. That is the tradition of the white shawl."

"I appreciate your sharing that with us," Blake said.

"Yes. Thank you," Nichelle said, staring down at the package in her arms.

"Let's get the bags from Olivia," Blake said. "Nichelle?"

She tore her gaze from the tissue-wrapped shawl. "What?"

"The fruit and veggies, remember?"

"Yes. Yes, of course." She spun around and started walking away quickly.

"Hey," Blake said, catching up with her in two long strides, "what's wrong? You like the shawl, don't you?"

"Oh, yes, it's lovely. It's just that . . . Never mind. I'm being silly."

"The tradition," he said, smiling. "You're all shook up over the tradition of the white shawl."

"I am not! Well, maybe just a tad. I mean, it's a nice tradition, but it's rather . . . personal."

"I like it." His smile grew bigger. "I'm really into that tradition stuff. Yes, sir, that's a top-notch, first-rate tradition. Do you know what grim, gross, gruesome things happen to people who break traditions?"

"I'm not listening to you."

"Don't forget," he said, suddenly serious, "you wear it only for your lover, the man you love. Don't forget that, Nichelle."

Before she could think of anything to say, Olivia called to them. They hurried to her booth.

"I'm closing soon," Olivia said. "I was afraid you'd forgotten your things. Did you have a nice day?"

"Oh, yes," Nichelle said. "It was really fun."

"I bought Nichelle a white shawl," Blake said, sounding extremely pleased with himself. Nichelle shot him a stormy glare.

"From Nina?" Olivia asked. "Did she tell you the tradition?"

"You bet," Blake said. "Every word."

"Did you remember Kurt and Eric's cantaloupe, Olivia?" Nichelle asked.

"That is such a romantic tradition," Olivia said dreamily.

Blake nodded. "Indeed it is."

"I hope the green grapes are sweet," Nichelle said.

"One mustn't break a Mexican tradition," Olivia said.

"Absolutely not," Blake said.

"Green grapes are better than the big purple ones," Nichelle said, "because the purple ones have seeds and Emily Post probably wouldn't approve of spitting them onto your plate. So, there you sit with a mouthful of seeds and . . ." Her voice trailed off as she realized that both Olivia and Blake were staring at her. "And stuff," she finished lamely.

"What are you babbling about?" Blake asked.

"Forget it. Just forget it. Olivia, may we have the sacks? I'll see you soon, okay?"

Olivia pulled the straw bags from beneath the stand, and Blake managed to juggle them both along with the chili bowls.

"I'll take something," Nichelle said.

"Nope, I'm all set."

"Ah, *muy macho,*" Olivia said, beaming.

"You'd better believe it," Blake said, wiggling his eyebrows. "It was great meeting you, Olivia. I hope I'll see you again soon."

"Oh, I'm sure that will happen. Good-bye, Nickie. Say hello to Kurt and Eric. And tell Marcella to call her poor old mother once in a while."

" 'Bye," Nichelle said, waving as she started away. "Come on, macho man." Blake chuckled and fell in step beside her.

Darkness descended like a heavy curtain over the city, but the multitude of lights brightened the sky. Traffic was heavy and Blake didn't speak as he concentrated on his driving. Nichelle sat quietly beside him, her hands resting on the tissue-wrapped shawl on her lap.

Wear it only for your lover, the man you love.

The words echoed over and over in her mind and heart. She would follow the tradition, she knew that. The question haunting her was whether or not she would wear the shawl for Blake Pemberton.

She looked over at him, studying his strong profile illuminated by the passing lights. She remembered seeing his magnificent body nearly nude that day in his apartment, and her heartbeat began to quicken. Her gaze drifted down to his powerful thighs, and heat poured through her as desire filled her.

Her fingers dug into the soft tissue and wool shawl. Would Blake ever come to love her? Was she already in love with *him*?

Oh, stop, she scolded herself. Nothing had changed. Blake was still out of her league, her world.

Oh, really? an inner voice taunted. *Then who was the handsome devil she'd spent the day with at the Pueblo?*

Yes, okay, she admitted. Blake had crossed over the line and left Bel Air far behind him to go to the Mexican village. He'd had a wonderful time, she was sure of it, and she had loved every minute they had shared. But one day did not a future make.

"Would you like to go out to dinner?" Blake asked.

She jumped. "What?"

"Didn't you know I was here?" he asked, flashing a grin at her.

"I was daydreaming."

"I asked if you wanted to go out to eat."

"No, thank you. I'm still full from all that food we ate."

"Oh."

"I could fix a fruit salad," she said quickly. Then he wouldn't leave right away.

"Sold," he said. He could stay for a while. Fantastic.

Blake carried her bags up to her apartment, and once inside headed straight for the kitchen. Nichelle stood alone in the living room, tightly clutching the delicate white shawl.

Six

Blake set the shopping bags on the kitchen counter and began to pull the fruit from one. He wasn't thinking about the fruit, though. The image of Nichelle was standing before him, the delicate white shawl draped around her shoulders.

She was beautiful, he thought. And he loved her.

Would she ever wear the shawl for him? he wondered. She'd been shaken by that tradition, but he knew she would follow it. Would he be her lover, the man she loved? Yes, dammit, he would. He had to be. Oh, God, he couldn't lose her now. She was his love, his life. Somehow he had to show her, convince her to love him in return.

Easy, Pemberton, he cautioned himself. He was panicking at the mere thought of losing Nichelle. He had to be patient, to watch for signs that he was chipping away at the wall she had built around herself. It was happening already as she slowly began to trust and believe in him. She'd shared a portion of herself with him when she'd told him that little bit about the life she'd led with her mother. And she'd allowed him to comfort her, to hold her when she cried.

Remembering the feel of her slender, warm body pressed against his sent a shot of desire through him. Suddenly he was filled with an ache to touch her, kiss her, to make her his. He wanted Nichelle in his bed. Becoming one with her would be an experience unlike any he'd ever had. The physical would intertwine with the emotional. It would be incredible, ecstatic. It would be—

"Blake?" Nichelle said.

"What!" he yelled, flipping a bunch of grapes into the air. They landed with a splat in the sink.

"I didn't mean to startle you," she said. "I'll make the salad."

"Yeah. Fine," he said gruffly, and snatched the grapes out of the sink.

"Is something wrong?"

He shook his head. "No." Everything would be just ducky, he thought, if she didn't drop her gaze below his belt. His body was going crazy at the idea of making love to Nichelle. Never in his life had he desired anyone the way he did her. Of course, that made sense, because he'd never been in love before. But, oh, merciful saints, how he wanted this woman.

"Hard," she said.

He snapped his head around to look at her. "What?" he croaked.

"This peach is hard. I thought I'd picked them out more carefully. Oh, well, I'll put it on the windowsill.

The sun will warm it, heat the natural juices, bring it up to perfection."

He plunked his elbows on the counter and sank his head into his hands. "Holy hell," he muttered. "I'm dying. Dying, I tell you. I can't take much more of this."

She set the peach on the counter and moved to his side. She placed her hand on his back, and his muscles tightened beneath her feathery touch.

"Blake, what is—"

"That's it," he said. He spun around, gripped her by the upper arms, and hauled her against him. "I'm kissing you." She stared at him with wide eyes. "Right this damn minute. Understand?"

"I—oh!"

His mouth swept down onto hers in a rough, urgent kiss that seemed to steal the very breath from her body. His hands slid to her back, then down over the slope of her buttocks, nestling her to him, against the evidence of his arousal.

Slowly the kiss gentled. He slid his tongue along her lower lip, then into her mouth to tease and taste, to heighten her passion. He leaned against the counter and spread his legs slightly, fitting her to him. Her knees went weak and she circled his neck with her arms, clinging to him for support. His hands roamed over her back, her buttocks, up along her ribs to the sides of her aching breasts. She moaned in pleasure.

He trailed kisses down her slender neck, his breathing raspy, his chest heaving. Then he claimed her mouth again, his tongue stroking hers possessively. Desire swirled within her like an uncontrolled fire, burning a path of passion straight through her. She pressed her hips more tightly to him, and he groaned deep in his chest.

With trembling hands he inched her sweater upward, then lifted his head. His gray eyes were smoky with passion, and wordlessly she raised her arms. He drew the sweater up and away, dropping it onto the floor. Her bra followed a moment later.

"Oh, Nichelle," he said hoarsely, "you're beautiful." He filled his palms with her small breasts, his thumbs brushing across the nipples. "Exquisite."

"Blake," she whispered as she savored the feel of his warm hands on her soft flesh.

"I won't hurt you," he said. "Do you trust me, Nichelle?"

"Yes. Oh, yes."

He dipped his head and drew the bud of one breast deep into his mouth, sucking with a rhythmic motion that matched the stroking of his thumb on her other breast. And matched the pulsing heat in the secret darkness of her womanhood. She arched her back to receive him, closing her eyes as wondrous sensations rocked through her. He paid homage to her other breast, and she felt as though she would shatter from the sheer pleasure of it all.

But still she wanted more.

She wanted Blake to fill her with his masculinity, to consume her with his virility and strength. To be complete, she must have him, all of him.

She loved him, she realized. Her body craved what her heart desired. "Blake," she gasped. "Please."

He lifted his head and drew a deep, shuddering breath. "I'm sorry," he said, his voice harsh with passion. "I didn't mean to go this far, but . . ."

"No." She gripped his shoulders. "Don't say that. I want you, Blake. I want you to make love to me."

He closed his eyes for a moment, clenching his jaw as he strove for control. "No," he said, looking at her again. "I can't. I seduced you, Nichelle. You're not thinking clearly or—" She pressed her lips firmly against his. "Oh, Lord," he groaned. "Don't do that. I want you so damn much."

"And I want you. I *am* thinking clearly. Love me, Blake. Please."

With a strangled moan he brought his mouth down hard on hers in a bruising kiss that she returned in kind. A moment later he lifted her into his arms and carried her from the kitchen into the bedroom. He set her on her feet and pulled her close, burying his face in her silken curls.

"Are you sure?" he asked. "I couldn't handle it if you were sorry afterward. I couldn't deal with it, Nichelle. Talk to me, tell me. Tell me again that this is what you want."

She smiled as an inner peace flooded through her, and she cupped his face in her hands. "I want you, Blake Pemberton," she whispered. "I want to be one with you."

His eyes searched hers, and she returned his gaze steadily, waiting for him to find the assurance he sought. At last he reached out and swept back the blankets on the bed.

Nichelle kicked off her shoes and he lifted her onto the cool sheets. Bracing his hands on either side of her head, he leaned over and kissed her deeply. Then he straightened and pulled off his sweater and shirt. He sat down next to her, and after one more searching look he reached for the snap on her jeans.

As he drew her jeans and panties down her legs, he kissed every inch of her dewy skin as it appeared. She was awash with desire as she clutched his shoulders. Her blood seemed to hum through her veins as he continued his tantalizing magic. His warm, seeking mouth moved upward again to find her breasts, then on to claim her mouth in a searing kiss. Finally he lifted his head, and his gaze swept over her naked body.

"You're like ivory," he said. "An ivory peach, or velvet, or . . . oh, Nichelle, you are really beautiful."

"You make me feel beautiful. You make me feel things I've never experienced before. I want you so much."

He stood and shed his remaining clothes. He saw her gaze travel over him, and he watched intently for any flicker of fear or hesitancy in her eyes. Instead, she smiled. It was a tender, womanly, welcoming smile, and an instant later he stretched out next to her and once more took possession of her mouth.

Nichelle trailed her hands over Blake's moist skin, tracing the lines of his muscles, twining her fingers in his curly chest hair. She pressed her lips to his shoulder to taste him, to inhale his masculine scent. He was magnificent. He was Blake, and she loved him. Nothing mattered but the moment, and what they were about to share. He slid his hand to the apex of her thighs, and she gasped.

"Oh, you do want me," he murmured against her lips. "I can feel how ready you are for me, Nichelle."

"Yes. Oh, yes. Now."

"It's going to be good," he went on, his voice strained. "I promise you. We're going to fly away together, Nichelle. You and me."

She tossed her head on the pillow. "Blake, please."

"So . . . damn . . . good," he said, and moved over her.

With a thrust of smooth, powerful heat he took her breath away. He filled her, pressing deep within her, touching her soul. Her eyes brimmed with tears at the sheer beauty of being one with Blake Pemberton.

"Nichelle? Am I hurting you?"

"No. Oh, no, never. It's wonderful."

"Then dance with me, love," he said huskily. "Go with me."

He moved slowly at first, watching her face, holding back, delaying the moment he so desperately ached for. But when she lifted her hips to bring him closer yet, his control snapped. The rhythm increased to a pounding cadence and they were one. In bodies, minds, and souls, they were one.

The raging rhythm carried them away, ever higher. Seeking. Striving. Struggling to the summit of their climb of rapture. And at last they reached it, and cried out to each other in ecstasy.

Blake collapsed on top of her, happily sated. Lord, how he loved her, he thought. He'd never felt so complete, so at peace. He wanted to tell her how he felt, declare his love, but knew he shouldn't. He didn't want to frighten her with too much at once. He'd treasure the gift she'd just given him, and wait.

He pushed himself up and smiled at her. "Hi."

"Hello," she said, matching his smile.

"Are you all right?"

"I've never been so all right in my entire life. I've

never experienced anything so wonderful, Blake. Thank you."

"Don't thank me. What we did, we did together. It's never been that good for me, Nichelle. I hope you believe me when I say that, because it's true. Am I too heavy? Should I get off you?"

"No, I like you right here," she said, wrapping her arms around his back.

"You don't look like you're sorry this happened. You don't act like you're sorry. But humor me, okay? Tell me, Nichelle. Let me hear the words."

"I'm not sorry, Blake Pemberton," she said softly. "I swear to you that I have no regrets." None at all, she reaffirmed in her mind. Falling in love with Blake was wrong, a dreadful mistake. But having made love with him was so right and good. Blake was still out of her reach, but nothing and no one could ever take her memories from her. "No regrets."

"Fantastic," he said, lowering his lips toward hers. "Absolutely fantastic."

The kiss was long and powerful, and her eyes widened as she felt his manhood stir with renewed desire within her.

"Blake?"

"I'll never get enough of you," he said, and nuzzled her neck. "Can you feel what you do to me?"

"Yes."

"You did that. It's all your fault."

She smiled. "I accept full responsibility."

And his love? he wondered. Would she come to accept his love? "Maybe we should wait awhile, let you recuperate. I don't want to hurt you."

"You're so considerate." She trailed her fingers down his back to his tight buttocks. "Such a gentleman." She outlined his mouth with the tip of her tongue and felt him shudder in response. "A real sweetheart of a guy." She arched her back to press her breasts more firmly to his chest.

With a throaty groan he claimed her mouth as he slid his arm beneath her hips to lift her to him. He drove farther within her, burying himself deeper in her silken heat that welcomed him fully. She whispered his name and matched his tempo beat for beat. Again they toppled over the edge into oblivion only seconds apart, then slowly drifted back.

When Blake moved away, he pulled the blankets over their cooling bodies, and she nestled close to him. She sighed in contentment, and within minutes drifted off to sleep. He watched her sleep as he gently sifted her curls through his fingers.

She looked so young lying there, he mused. So young and fragile and enchanting. He loved her so much. . . .

Suddenly he remembered the white shawl. Well, he'd made it to step one, he thought. He was Nichelle's lover. But he wasn't the man she loved. At least, she hadn't said anything about loving him, but then he loved her and hadn't told her. Maybe that wasn't such a hot idea. Love should be based on honesty and trust.

So, okay, he'd tell Nichelle that he loved her. He'd figured she wasn't ready to hear those words yet, but since when was he such an expert on how women's minds worked? He'd say, "Hey, Nichelle, what's doin'? By the way, I love you." Not good. "Nichelle, I love you. I'm not saying that because we went to bed together." Oh, hell. Forget it. He wouldn't rehearse it, but would just wing it. He'd watch for the right moment, and then just tell her. Check.

With a satisfied nod he smoothed the blankets over her shoulders, closed his eyes, and went to sleep.

Nichelle stirred. She couldn't move! Then she realized she was being held tightly in Blake's arms. The room was dark and she turned her head to look at the clock on the nightstand. Eight-ten. She hadn't slept very long, but she felt totally refreshed, and definitely hungry. She moved carefully out of his arms and slipped off the bed. After a quick shower she rubbed the steam from the mirror and peered at her reflection.

Heaven above, she thought, leaning closer. Her eyes were dancing a jig. They were sparkling, for Pete's sake. She looked older, too, she was sure of it, more mature, more womanly. Making love with Blake certainly agreed with her.

She pulled on her blue terry-cloth robe and walked back into the bedroom. After waiting a moment for her eyes to adjust to the darkness, she crossed to the edge of the bed and gazed at Blake.

I love you, she whispered silently.

With a gentle smile on her lips she left the room and went into the kitchen to make the fruit salad. A half an hour later she heard the water running in the shower, and ten minutes after that Blake appeared in the kitchen. He was wearing his jeans and shirt, but the shirt was unbuttoned and hanging free. Her heart skipped a beat at the sight of him.

He smiled. "Hi."

She smiled back. "Hi. Hungry?"

He circled her waist with his arms and nuzzled her neck. "Always. I'm always hungry. What's on the menu?"

"Fruit salad," she said breathlessly as a shiver coursed through her. "Quit nibbling on the cook."

"You taste good. Smell good too. Let's go back to bed."

"Oh, but I'm weak from hunger," she said dramatically. "Fading away to a mere shadow of my former self. Pour the coffee."

He chuckled. "Check."

She placed a large bowl of salad on the table, along with a plate of hot buttery toast. They sat opposite each other and Blake peered into the bowl.

"Okay, let's see," he said. "Peaches, grapes, cantaloupe . . ." He glanced up at Nichelle, who was also looking into the bowl. "Bananas. I love you, Nichelle."

"Watermelon too, and—" She snapped her head up to meet his eyes. "What?"

He took her hands in his. "I love you."

"No," she said, shaking her head. "No, you don't."

He smiled. "Yes, I do. I really love you. I, Blake Pemberton, am in love with you, Nichelle Clay."

"But you can't be." She jerked her hands free as she felt the color drain from her face. "No."

Blake's smile was replaced by a frown. "Hey, calm down, okay? Maybe I shouldn't have told you in the middle of the grapes and bananas, but it's true, I do love you. I don't understand why you're so upset. How I feel about you can't be *that* much of a surprise."

"Of course it's a surprise," she said, jumping to her feet. She sat back down again as her trembling legs refused to support her. "You never fall in love.

You have lots of women. There's Miss Six-and-a-half-narrow and . . . you don't have to say you love me just because we . . ."

"Knock it off," he said, smacking the table with his hand. "I have never—Are you listening to me? —never before in my entire life told a woman that I love her. Until now. Until you. I love you. You've got a helluva lot of nerve insinuating that I'm feeding you a line." He crossed his arms over his chest and slouched back in his chair, scowling at her.

"I don't want you to love me," she said, her voice trembling.

"That's too damn bad, because I already do. This is not how this conversation was supposed to go. Why am I being made to feel like a villain here? Would you mind explaining why you don't want me to love you?"

"Because—because we're wrong for each other."

"You didn't think so when we were in bed together."

"That has nothing to do with this," she said, her voice rising.

"Oh, really? What was that then? A quick roll in the hay? A little exercise because you missed your aerobics class or something?"

"Stop it. Don't you dare cheapen what we shared!"

"Damn right, I won't." He leaned forward and pierced her with his keen gaze. "Because it was special, and it was you and me." His tone softened. "And because I love you. Nichelle, I don't expect you to love me yet, but I wanted you to know how I feel. Don't run from me, leprechaun. There's nothing for you to be frightened of."

"Blake, please," she said, clutching her hands tightly in her lap, "you don't understand. Or you refuse to.

We come from different worlds, we have nothing in common. We don't belong together. I'm your cleaning lady, remember? You move in a social climate I don't want any part of. I won't cross over that line, Blake. I won't."

Blood pounded against his temples. Dammit, he raged inwardly, he'd blown it. He'd rushed her and scared her to death. If only he had all the pieces to the puzzle of her past. He couldn't fight ghosts when he didn't know the whole story. He had to calm down, regroup. And wait.

"Okay," he said, releasing a long breath. "You don't want to hear that I love you, so I won't say it. As of now, you're my 'significant other.' How's that? I am also, Miss Clay, your lover. We'll take this slow and easy."

"Oh, Blake," she said, sighing, "I don't know what to do. The best thing would be for you to leave now and not come back."

"Is that what you want?" he asked, his voice low. "Truth, Nichelle. Is it?"

"No," she whispered. "I thought . . . I hoped we might have a little time together. Not a future, but a little time."

"How much is a little?" he asked, narrowing his eyes.

She threw up her hands. "I don't know. I'm so confused."

"Have a grape. You'll feel better." He ladled a serving of salad onto her plate, then did the same to his own. "Eat."

"I'm not hungry."

"Now I've made you lose your appetite? You don't

do much for a guy's ego." He took a bite of salad. "Delicious. Try it."

Nichelle picked up her fork and pushed the fruit around on her plate. When Blake cleared his throat, she forced herself to take a bite.

"That's a good girl." She glared at him. "Nichelle, look, we'll back up, okay? I can't change how I feel about you, but I won't shove it at you every two minutes. We'll be together, have a good time, see what happens. That's a fair compromise, I think. You don't really want to dust me off, and I won't declare my undying love. Agreed?"

"Well, I guess so."

"Great. Eat another grape. They apparently do wonderful things for your brain."

She shot him another stormy glare, but resumed eating.

Oh, man! Blake thought. Talk about skating on thin ice. When he screwed things up, he really did a job of it. His announcement that he loved her had been about as welcome as an IRS audit. He was hanging on by a thread, but he *was* hanging on. He'd bought some time. How much, he didn't know, so he'd better make every minute count.

Different worlds, he mused. Nichelle was really hung up on that. It had something to do with her mother. And her father?

Nichelle ate her salad without tasting it, and kept her eyes averted from Blake. He loved her, her mind repeated over and over. Blake Pemberton was in love with her. Or so he said. No, he meant it, he really loved her. Oh, why did he have to go and fall in love with her? It was bad enough that she loved him.

But now, when their time together was over, he'd be hurt, and she didn't want that.

And it *would* be over, their time. If she were stronger, she'd send him away now, but she couldn't. Not yet.

A knock sounded at the door.

"That's probably Eric," she said, starting to rise. "He knows Olivia will have sent a cantaloupe for him and Kurt."

"Stay put," Blake said, and stood up. "I'll answer the door. You don't know for sure that it's Eric."

But it was.

Eric stepped into the apartment, immediately noticed Blake's unbuttoned shirt and bare feet, and folded his arms over his massive chest. Eric definitely was not smiling.

"Maybe I misjudged you, Pemberton," he said in a low, menacing voice.

"Maybe it's none of your damn business," Blake said in the same tone.

"Nickie's happiness *is* my business. I thought I made that clear."

"She's a woman, not a child. She can make her own decisions. Buzz off, Franklin. You're overstepping this time. This is between Nichelle and me. But for the record, I have no intention of hurting her."

"Yes, you will," Eric said, taking a step toward him. "You're uptown big bucks. Nickie can't handle that, don't you see?"

"No, dammit, I don't see. I can't get all the facts from her, just bits and pieces. What happened to her, Eric? What am I up against? What am I fighting?"

"If she wanted you to know, she'd tell you. Since

she's chosen not to, I want you to haul it out of here. Stay away from her, Pemberton. I'm not saying it again."

"Blake," Nichelle said, coming into the room, "who was—oh, hi, Eric. Olivia sent a cantaloupe for you and Kurt."

"Fine," Eric said. His angry glare was still locked with Blake's, but then he glanced at Nichelle. When he saw her robe, his attention snapped back to Blake. "Damn you."

"Eric, don't," Nichelle said, hurrying over to the two of them.

Eric raked his hand through his hair. "What have you done, Nickie? Pemberton is wrong for you, you know that."

"I'm warning you, Franklin," Blake said. "Butt . . . out. Now!"

"I'm going to take you apart, Pemberton!"

"Stop it," Nichelle snapped, stepping between them. "Both of you, stop it. You sound like little boys fussing over a toy. Blake, Eric is merely concerned about my welfare."

"He's pushing it," Blake roared. "And me! He has nothing to do with us, Nichelle."

"The hell I don't," Eric bellowed.

"Eric, shut up," Nichelle said, tilting her head back to glare up at him.

"Me?" Eric said, shocked.

"Yeah, you," Blake said sullenly.

"And you," Nichelle said, poking Blake in the chest. "Put a cork in it. Now, listen to me, both of you. I don't need this hassle. I can't handle it. Not now. You either call a truce or I'll refuse to speak to either one of you. I mean it. I'll become a recluse, a female

Howard Hughes. I'll join a nunnery. I'll buy an answering machine for my phone and never respond to a knock at my door. I'll be a persona non grata."

"A what?" Eric asked.

"Or whatever," she said, shrugging.

Blake chuckled. "You're a nut case, Clay."

"And you two are pushing me over the edge!" she shouted.

"I'm sorry, Nickie," Eric said, looking at the toe of his shoe.

"Thank you," she said primly. "Mr. Pemberton?"

"Yeah, okay, I'm sorry," he said, running his hand across the back of his neck. "But this guy has no right to—"

"Blake!"

"Oh, hell," he said, and stalked over to the window.

Nichelle stomped into the kitchen, returned with a cantaloupe, and shoved it at Eric.

"Go home," she said.

"What about him?" Eric asked, glancing at Blake's broad back.

"He's *my* problem," Nichelle said.

"That's no joke. He's a problem, all right. A big one. I'll be around, Nickie. You can count on it."

"Good-bye, Eric."

Eric closed the door behind him, and a silence fell over the room. Nichelle stared at the rigid set to Blake's shoulders, and felt her burst of bravado fade into oblivion. He turned slowly to face her.

"Would you like a dish of ice cream?" she asked, smiling brightly. "It's mint chocolate chip. Great stuff. Green, with specks of chocolate."

"No," he said, walking slowly toward her.

"Oh. How about a sugar cookie?"

"No."

"Right."

"You seem a bit nervous." He stopped in front of her.

"Of course I'm nervous. You just crossed the room like a panther about to leap on a helpless victim."

He laughed. "Nichelle, you're about as helpless as an army regiment. You just took on two men who outweigh you by over a hundred pounds each, and won. You're a scary lady when you get going."

"I am?" she asked, smiling. "I'll be darned."

"You are also," he said, his voice low as he cradled her face in his hands, "the most beautiful, fascinating, fantastic woman I have ever known." He lowered his lips toward hers and they forgot all about mint chocolate chip ice cream.

Seven

On Monday afternoon Nichelle sat staring out the window of the bus that was making its way slowly across town. She had an appointment with her accountant, but her mind was not on tax forms. Only one thought, one image, danced through her thoughts: Blake Pemberton.

She smiled. Frowned. Sighed. Then smiled again. Her emotions were not, she admitted, very consistent when it came to Blake and the precarious state of her relationship with him. The smile, she knew, was due to the glorious weekend they had spent making love, going for walks, watching old movies on TV. And making love, making love, making love.

The intermittent frowns were caused by the distressing facts that kept creeping into her mind and bringing her back to reality. She was deeply in love with the wrong man.

She sighed. Again. The sighs were a mixture. Some

were from happiness as she relived the weekend, and some were from sadness as she thought that everything she had with Blake would end, and she would once more be alone.

Alone. She tested the word out, and a chill settled in her soul. She hadn't felt alone since moving to Los Angeles and gaining Eric's and Kurt's friendship. Her newfound family had grown with Marcella, Olivia, the other leprechauns, and so many others. She'd viewed her life as being rich and full. She had financial security, everything she needed.

Until now. Until having fallen in love with Blake Pemberton. When Blake was gone the others would still be there, but there would be a void, an empty place in her life without him.

He had kept his word. He had not mentioned his love for her again during the rest of the weekend. But she had seen it in his eyes, his smile, felt it in his touch. After she'd placed the white shawl, still wrapped in the tissue paper, on her closet shelf, she had turned to find him gazing at her longingly. But he didn't know, would never know, that she could wear the shawl for him and follow the shawl's tradition.

When he had left late last night, she had lain in bed picturing him driving away, across the line that took him out of her reach. They had stayed in her part of town the entire weekend, but then it had been time for him to go back to where he really belonged.

"I'll call you tomorrow," he had said as he dressed.

"All right."

He sat down on the edge of the bed and smiled at her. "These have been two wonderful days, Nichelle."

"Yes. Yes, they have," she said, placing her hand on his cheek.

"The first of hundreds, thousands."

"Blake . . ."

"Shh, I'm kissing you."

He'd left her tingling with desire and with a smile on her lips. When she finally slept, she'd hugged his pillow, which still faintly smelled of him, and dreamed of him until waking at dawn.

She was startled from her reverie when she saw they were near her stop, and quickly signaled the driver. The air was heavy with smog and her eyes were burning by the time she'd walked the half block to the building where her accountant's office was.

She looked classy, Nichelle decided, glancing at her reflection in the glass doors. Very businesslike. Her rust sweater, rust and brown tweed wool skirt, and brown heels were right on the mark. She just hoped to the heavens there was no hint in her eyes or on her face that she'd made mad, passionate love all weekend. How embarrassing!

Her accountant was a tall, attractive woman in her forties, who had sleek dark hair and a ready smile. But not today. Diane Watson was frowning as she waved Nichelle into the chair opposite her desk.

"Am I in trouble?" Nichelle asked.

"I did your taxes," Diane said. "You owe a bundle, but you have it, and more, in your savings. But, Nichelle, this is ridiculous. You don't have any deductions worth speaking of. I don't suppose you could have six kids before we file this? No, forget that. Listen to me, you have got to invest some of your funds."

"You've told me that before," Nichelle said. "That

makes me very nervous. My money would be tied up and I couldn't get at it in an emergency. Or I might invest in the wrong thing and lose it all."

"Nichelle, you're in a tax bracket now that is taking a tremendous bite out of your income. You can have your emergency fund, but you also must put some of your cash to work for you. As for what to invest in, there are professionals who specialize in advising people in such matters."

"Blake," Nichelle said, nodding.

"Who?"

"Blake Pemberton. He's . . . a friend of mine who owns an investment company."

"Pemberton Investments?" Diane asked. "I've heard of them. Great reputation. Good. Go see this Blake and tell him you want to invest twenty-five thousand dollars."

"What!" Nichelle yelled, jumping to her feet. "Twenty-five what?"

"Sit. Look at these forms." Diane pushed a stack of papers across the desk. "You have enough in your emergency fund to cover your expenses for months. The twenty-five thousand can be invested, made to earn more for you, while possibly saving you some tax dollars. Pemberton Investments will steer you in the right direction."

Nichelle picked up the papers and slouched back in her chair, frowning as she carefully scrutinized the forms. She wanted to sigh, decided she'd used up her quota while thinking of Blake, then sighed anyway.

"Oh," she said for lack of anything better to say.

"Very profound," Diane said, finally smiling. "Do you understand what I'm saying?"

"Yes, it's all quite clear. But twenty-five thousand dollars?"

"Leprechauns, Inc., is doing splendidly, you know that. I pay you a great deal of money to have my apartment cleaned and my cupboards kept full with food, and it's worth every penny. You're a highly successful businesswoman, Nichelle, whether you want to face that fact or not."

"What do you mean?"

"I don't know exactly. You're the only client I have who tries to pretend nothing has changed in her financial status. You're still living at the same address, which doesn't reflect your income, and you resist even acknowledging how far you've come. It's my duty as your accountant to advise you to make some sound investments immediately. If you know Blake Pemberton, then you're all set. Do it, Nichelle. Put yourself in Blake Pemberton's hands."

If she only knew, Nichelle thought dryly, how many times during the past weekend she'd put herself in Blake's hands. "I'll think about it," she said, getting to her feet. She slipped the papers into her briefcase, then extended her hand to Diane. "Thank you."

Diane shook her hand. "Would you like me to call and make an appointment for you at Pemberton Investments?" she asked hopefully.

"No. No, I'll do it. I will. Good-bye, Diane, and thanks again."

"Invest that money," Diane called after her.

Outside the building Nichelle decided to walk to sort through all that Diane had said. She should be thrilled, she supposed, that Leprechauns, Inc., was doing so well. But, oh, darn, it was frightening. She didn't want to move to a better neighborhood, or make fancy investments. One step led to the next, down a road she didn't wish to travel, closer to the line she had no desire to cross over.

But Diane was right, of course. Investments, proper investments, could be added security for the future. But then again . . . darn it, what should she do? Maybe if she talked to Blake about this she'd have a better idea of just what kind of investments were available to her and, she hoped, would feel more comfortable about the whole thing. Yes, okay, she'd talk to him.

She realized that her new pumps were killing her feet and sat down on the bench at the next bus stop she came to. A short time later she was headed home, still deep in thought about her finances. The telephone was ringing when she entered her apartment.

"Hello?"

"Hi."

She smiled instantly. "Blake?"

"Yep. I was going to leave a message with your answering service if you weren't there. I'm glad I caught you."

"So am I. I need to talk to you."

"I'm listening," he said in a low, sexy tone of voice.

"No, I mean on a professional basis. I've just come from seeing my accountant and . . . it's all very complicated. Should I make an appointment to speak with you at your office?"

"You bet. We'll make love on top of my desk."

"Blake!"

"No, huh? Damn. Your accountant thinks you need to invest some money?"

"Yes," she said miserably.

He chuckled. "I can tell you're thrilled. Look, why don't I bring over some Chinese food, and I'll take a look at the situation. Do you have your tax forms?"

"Yes."

"Six-thirty?"

"Yes, all right."

"Cheer up, my sweet. Spending money is easy once you get the hang of it. See you soon."

"Blake, I insist on paying you for your time."

"We'll work something out. Gotta go. 'Bye."

"Good-bye," she said, and slowly replaced the receiver. "Spending money is easy once you get the hang of it," she repeated. Oh, how well she knew that that was true. First came the credit cards. Then you spent money you didn't have. Then . . . "Lord, I hate this. I really hate this."

After finishing her business for the day Nichelle soaked in a leisurely Mr. Bubble bubble bath and nearly fell asleep. She had just finished dressing in tan cords and a red turtleneck when Blake arrived.

"Dinnertime," he said, heading straight for the kitchen. "Get it while it's hot."

She followed behind him, her gaze sweeping over his jeans and steel-gray sweater that showed off his muscled physique wonderfully—and wreaked total havoc with her heart rate.

"First things first," he said as he set two large white bags on the table. He pulled her into his arms. "Hi."

He kissed her thoroughly, and she was slightly dizzy when he released her.

"Hello," she said breathlessly.

"Let's eat, I'm starved. Then we'll talk business."

"We don't have to," she said, taking two plates out

of the cupboard. "After all, you worked all day. You probably aren't in the mood to discuss investments in the evening too. No problem. I'll call your secretary and make an appointment for next week. Yes, that's a much better idea."

"Hold it," he said, raising his hand. "Slow down. You're talking a hundred miles an hour. Does the thought of investing some money upset you this much?"

She sat down at the table. "It's not just the money. It's the overall picture of what it represents."

He began removing small white cartons from the bags. "Just what does it represent?" he asked, striving for a casual tone.

"A way of life, a beginning of a pattern of living. Oh, I don't know, Blake, it's hard for me to explain. If a person is happy in the existence he's created for himself, why should he tamper with it?"

"Are you?" he asked quietly. "Happy?"

She opened her mouth to answer yes, then clamped it shut again. Yes, she was happy, she told herself. Then she imagined what her days and nights would be like when Blake was gone. There was no hint of happiness. Darn, it seemed as though every part of her life was topsy-turvy since she'd beamed down into Blake Pemberton's bedroom as a green-haired alien. Nothing was as it used to be.

"Sure, I'm happy," she said brightly. "Mmm, everything smells good. I adore Chinese food."

"Dig in," Blake said, opening a box. She was really shook up, he thought. He'd never met anyone who fought change the way Nichelle did, at least no one as young as she. She was scared to death of . . . of what? She had a fixation about security. That made sense after hearing the grim tale of flights in the night to escape bill collectors. What he didn't have a handle on was her preoccupation with staying where she said she belonged, not wanting to take one step forward toward a better standard of living. He had to have more pieces to the puzzle.

"This is delicious," she said. "Thank you. I haven't had Chinese food in ages. My mother detested it. She said if we were meant to eat Chinese food, we'd be living in China."

This was the opening he'd been waiting for. *Don't blow it.* "Did she say the same thing about Mexican food?"

"No, she loved tacos. I'd make them for her often. Especially toward the end, when she didn't have much of an appetite. I'd tempt her with homemade tacos."

"How did she die?"

"Her heart. She was bedridden for the last year."

"And you took care of her?"

"Yes. We lived in a duplex and the woman on the other side would look in while I worked."

"There wasn't anything the doctors could do?"

"No. There's no cure for a broken heart."

"What?" he asked, leaning toward her.

"Oh, they had a fancy name for what was wrong with my mother, but they didn't know the facts like *I* did. All those years that she spent pretending, hoping, dreaming that he'd— May I have an egg roll, please?"

"Sure." He handed the box to her. Damn, now what? Should he push for more answers, or give it a rest? No, he'd press a bit and hope Nichelle didn't freak out. "Who broke your mother's heart?" he asked, looking directly at her. His thundering heartbeat was echoing in his ears.

"My"—she took a deep breath, then released it—"father."

"Go on," he said gently. "You said he'd been gone for a long time. I assumed he'd died."

"Oh, no, he's very much alive. He's an important man in San Diego. I'm sure his name has been in the Los Angeles papers, too, but I prefer to watch the news on television rather than read the papers. That way I won't have to deal with seeing stories about how wonderful he is."

"I don't recall any glowing articles about someone named Clay."

"That's not his name," she said, lifting her chin. "You see, he never married my mother. Even when he knew she was pregnant with me, he wouldn't marry her. He's never seen or spoken to me."

"My God," Blake said, grasping her hand. "I'm sorry. Damn, that really stinks."

"I don't care about him. It's what it did to my mother. For over twenty years she believed he'd come for us. She kept going to where she knew he'd be and . . . I can't talk about this anymore. I don't know why I even started on this subject."

"Because I care, because I was listening, because your pain is my pain." Because he loved her.

"You're a very nice man, Blake Pemberton," Nichelle whispered, fighting back her tears.

A soothing silence fell between them as they stared at each other. But then the mood slowly changed as within both of them desire flickered from an ember to a flame. Their need, their want, was there. And the heat. Burning.

"Nichelle," Blake said, his voice raspy, "what you do to me."

"I feel it too."

"Eat your egg roll, before I say the hell with dinner and carry you into the bedroom."

"Can we vote?"

"No. I'm not having you skipping meals because I can't keep my hands off you. Eat."

"Blake, does it bother you that I'm—"

"Nichelle, don't you dare insult me by asking if your being illegitimate bothers me. Don't even think it. Got that?"

"Goodness," she said, smiling, "you're certainly ferocious all of a sudden."

"You all of a sudden insulted me."

"I'm sorry."

"I should hope so. My great-grandfather's second cousin was hanged for cattle rustling. Does that bother *you*?"

She laughed. "No."

"I rest my case. The only thing that matters here is us, you and me. That's it." She was smiling again, he thought. He'd better drop the subject of her parents for now. He had more pieces to the puzzle. Not all of them yet, but more. Lord, her father sounded like scum. "Want some fried rice?" he asked.

They continued to eat as they chatted about a new movie that was getting mixed reviews, and a labor leader who was scheduled to speak at UCLA. Nichelle finally said she couldn't eat another bite, then groaned when Blake asked for a bowl of the mint chocolate chip ice cream.

"Ahh," he said, peering into his bowl, "and to think I met you when your hair was this color."

She laughed. "I didn't have chocolate chips in my hair. It was a very even green. I'll put the rest of this food in the refrigerator while you eat that."

"Then we'll get serious. You see before you, madam, one of the best investment counselors in the city of Los Angeles."

"Whoop-dee-do," she said. "Just what I always wanted."

He laughed, then gave his undivided attention to his ice cream.

Nichelle busied herself putting away the food as she thought of all she had told Blake about herself. No one but Kurt, Eric, and Marcella knew about her father. Yet she had wanted Blake to know who she was, what she was. What had she been trying to do? Give him an out, a reason to gasp in horror and bolt for the door? No, he'd reacted just as she'd anticipated—calm, a flash of anger at her father's callousness, then acceptance. She'd simply wanted him to know because she loved him.

Granted, she'd left out a lot of the story—the pain she'd felt at her mother's behavior, the lessons she had learned. But her mother was dead, and Nichelle had no desire to tarnish her memory further by recounting all those years. It was over. Her mother was at last at peace.

Nichelle knew she was wrong in loving Blake, but she would face the ramifications of walking away from that love later. Later.

"Delicious mint chocolate chip," Blake said, putting his bowl into the sink. "You really know how to serve up a fine bowl of mint chocolate chip, Nichelle. I can't remember when I've had such great mint—"

"Blake?"

"Yeah?"

"Shut up."

"Got it."

He grabbed her hand and hauled her out of the kitchen. He sat on the sofa, pulled her onto his lap, then dipped her back over his arm.

"I'm doing a survey," he said, his lips a fraction of an inch from hers.

"Oh?" she said, hardly breathing.

"I need to determine if you taste better than mint chocolate chip."

She was delicious, he decided an instant later. She went limp in his arms as his tongue met hers. She slid her fingers to the nape of his neck as his hand crept beneath her turtleneck to find her breast. His head snapped up.

"You're not wearing a bra," he said.

"Sad part is"—she sighed dramatically—"you couldn't tell the difference."

"Now I can. Oh, lady, now I definitely can."

He took possession of her mouth once more as his thumb stroked the tip of her breast to a taut hardness. He trailed his hand across her skin, igniting a heated path as he went. He sought and found her other breast, which was aching for his magical touch. She arched into his hand, and he groaned as his arousal pressed against her.

"Don't wiggle," he murmured.

She wiggled. He moaned.

"Where are your tax forms?" he asked, his voice raspy.

"Is that a kinky question?" She flicked her tongue along his lower lip.

"You're not going to postpone discussing business by seducing me, Miss Clay."

"Oh, okay." She slid her hand beneath his sweater and inched her fingers upward, tangling them in the hair on his chest. He sucked in his breath. "I'll get my tax forms."

"What you're going to get," he said, lunging to his feet with her in his arms, "is me!"

"Hooray," she yelled, and he laughed as he strode into the bedroom.

There, amusement faded and desire reigned supreme. Clothes seemed to float away, then Blake pulled her down onto the bed with him. She lay on top of him, feeling surrounded by his heat, his strength. He gripped her waist to bring her higher, to give him access to her breasts. He sucked one, then the other, and a soft purr of pleasure escaped from her throat. She moved her hips in a tantalizing motion, and felt the shudder of response rip through him.

"Don't . . . wiggle," he said, then shifted her to claim her mouth in a deep, passionate kiss.

His hands skimmed over her back in restless frenzy, then wandered down to her buttocks, fitting her to him, holding her close to his pulsing heat.

"Blake, please," she gasped, tearing her mouth from his. "Now. Please."

In one smooth, powerful motion, he rolled her beneath him and entered her, filling her, consuming her, making them one. He thundered within her and she urged him on, matching his tempo, calling his name. Their loving was rough, urgent. It was heaven. They scaled the heights as ecstasy rocketed through their bodies.

"Blake!"

"Yes!"

He collapsed against her, then rolled onto his back, holding her tightly to him.

"Nichelle," he gasped. "You're incredible."

"So are you," she said, nestling her head on his shoulder. "Do I beat out mint chocolate chip?"

"I may have to gather further data on the subject."

"Marvelous," she said dreamily.

They lay quietly, sated and peaceful and very close to drifting off to sleep. Suddenly Blake stiffened.

"Oh, no, you don't," he said. "You had your wicked way with me, but I'm wise to your methods now. Get off my body and go get your tax forms."

"No."

"Go."

"What a dud," she said, then began to slide provocatively down his body.

"Nope. No way." He lifted her up and plopped her on her back next to him. "Behave yourself."

"Well!" she said indignantly, then crawled off the bed and stomped from the room.

He watched her leave. "That's one of the sweetest exits I've ever seen," he said under his breath.

When she returned to the bedroom, he had pulled up the blankets and propped the pillows against the headboard.

"Come into my office, Miss Clay," he said, patting the space next to him. She laughed and did as instructed. He tucked the sheet over her breasts. "You disturb my superior concentration. Now, let's see what's what."

Nichelle watched as he slowly and meticulously studied the stack of papers. At one point he whistled low and long, but made no further comment. The minutes ticked by, and she began to chew on the inside of her cheek. Finally he lowered the papers and stared straight ahead.

"I had no idea your business was this successful."

"Oh, well . . ." she shrugged.

He turned to look at her. "Your accountant is right. From what I see here, if you want to be conservative, you could safely invest twenty to twenty-five thousand. If you're going for the gusto, you could push it to maybe thirty, thirty-five. Forty thousand max."

"No. That's far too much. Diane said twenty-five, and that's scary enough."

"It really isn't. It's smart money management. If it's done with finesse, precise timing."

"I don't understand all that stuff," she said, frowning.

"You don't have to. That's what I'm here for. There's no question in my mind as to what you should do."

"Oh?"

"Buy a house."

"What?" she said, her eyes wide. "Are you crazy? What would I do with a house?"

"Live in it, of course, and save yourself a bundle of money in taxes."

"I can't afford a house."

"Yes, you can. You go cash to mortgage, pick up a low interest rate, and your payment stays within your range. You can make one bedroom into an office for Leprechauns, Inc., and take that as a business expense. You can always sell the house later, make a profit, and get a bigger place. Onward and upward, and all that good jazz." It would do for a start, he thought. It would get her used to the idea of leaving this neighborhood.

"No," she said. "I don't want to buy a house."

"Well, you don't have to do it in the next five minutes. Think about it a while."

"No."

He frowned. "Come on, Nichelle, you're not being reasonable. There are other investments available to you, but I really think a house is your best bet."

"I like it here," she said, folding her arms over her breasts.

"No, you feel safe here. There's a big difference between the two. Listen to me. There's nothing out there to frighten you. You'd enjoy having your own little place. You've worked hard, and it's time to reap some of the rewards from that labor. You don't belong in this neighborhood anymore."

"Yes, I do," she said, scrambling to her knees, the sheet forgotten as it slipped away. "This is exactly where I belong." Tears filled her eyes and her voice trembled. "Everything I want and need is here."

"I don't live here," he said quietly, looking directly at her.

"I know that, but you come here to be with me. Everything is fine just the way it is, don't you see?"

"No, it's not," he said, gripping her shoulders. "You're hiding in this place. You can have better. You deserve better. You told me that Eric and Kurt are trying to get out of here. Why not you?"

"No!" she cried, shrilly. "I won't cross over that line. I won't try to be what I'm not. I have money now, but who's to say I'll have it tomorrow? There's no guarantee, no promises made that mean anything."

"Dammit," he said, shaking her slightly, "I've promised to love you until the day I die. Are you saying you don't believe me? That you think I'm feeding you a bunch of bull?"

"No, I believe that you love me, and I love you, and—"

"What?"

"But it doesn't matter because—"

"What did you say? Nichelle, do you love me? Do you?"

"Yes, dammit!" She sobbed then, tears streaming down her cheeks. "But it isn't going to change anything."

"Oh, Nichelle." He pulled her to his chest and held her close. "Nichelle, Nichelle. You love me. I can't believe it. The white shawl. You'll wear the white shawl for me. Me!"

"You're not listening to me," she said, trying to break free. He tightened his hold on her.

"Shh, calm down," he said gently. "Just take it easy, okay? Don't cry. Are you calm?"

"No."

"I'll wait," he said, rubbing her back. "I'll sit here, hold you, and wait."

Several minutes passed in total silence as he continued stroking her back. She loved him, he thought exultantly. She did! They'd tackle everything together now, solve the problems, plan their future. She would come to believe in him, trust in his promise of love. Lord, he'd like to get his hands on that father of hers. The man had left deep scars on a child he'd never acknowledged. But there was still more to this than just Nichelle's father. There were pieces still missing from the puzzle.

She took a deep breath, then lifted her head to look at him. "I'm calm now."

"Okay," he said, smiling. "You're also beautiful, and I love you. I'm going to say that all the time now, because I know you love me. You're not alone, Nichelle. I'm going to be with you always. You've got to believe that."

She shifted to rest her back against the headboard, pulling the sheet up over her breasts again.

"I didn't intend to tell you that I love you," she said softly.

"Why not?" he asked, nestling one of her hands in his.

"Because it just won't work for us. I can't, won't leave here, Blake. And I don't mean just this apartment. I'm talking about my world, my space. You belong in Bel Air. You were comfortable in that fancy restaurant we went to, but I felt like Cinderella waiting for the clock to chime. And time does run out; everything catches up with the person who tries to be what she really isn't."

"Sweetheart, you've earned your way out of here. You're not pretending to be what you're not. You're Nichelle Clay, founder and president of Leprechauns, Inc. You're an intelligent, hardworking businesswoman. And you are loved by a man who wants to devote his life to making you happy. Please don't hide behind your walls anymore. We can have so much together. So very much."

Fresh tears sprang to her eyes as she looked at him. She wanted to fling her arms around his neck, tell him over and over how much she loved him, assure him they would be together forever.

But the words wouldn't come.

Images from the past cast shadows over this man and the future, pushing him further and further from her reach.

"Marry me, Nichelle," he said. "Marry me."

In a whisper so soft Blake could hardly hear her, Nichelle said one word that carried the force of a painful blow to his body.

"No."

Eight

At noon the next day Blake absently nodded his thanks to the waitress who refilled his coffee cup for the umpteenth time, never taking his eyes off the door of the restaurant. He had arrived earlier than the agreed-upon hour, which had been a mistake. He was a wreck. Cool, professional investment expert Blake Pemberton was coming apart at the seams.

He took a deep breath, released it slowly, decided it hadn't helped a bit, and scowled. His mind skittered back to the scene the previous night in Nichelle's apartment, and a knot tightened in his stomach.

"No," he heard her say again. "No." Such a small word, and she had spoken it barely above a whisper. But it had held a tone of finality that had told him the wall she was hiding behind was stronger than ever.

He hadn't known what to say or do, so he'd held her close and finally told her that they'd forget about it for now. She had looked tired, totally worn out, and he had told her he'd leave, and had promised to call her the next day. She'd forced a smile, sighed, then closed her eyes and fallen asleep. He had sat by the bed watching her sleep for the next hour, then had quietly left the apartment.

Blake pressed the heels of his hands to his eyes. He'd hardly slept through the long hours of the night. He was going to lose his Nichelle, he knew it, and the realization was whipping him into a combined state of frustration, anger, and cold fear.

He looked at the door again, then stiffened. Eric was here. Blake stood up and watched Eric cross the room, seeing the appreciative glances the handsome, well-built man received from the women in the restaurant.

Damn, he was big, Blake thought. If Eric decided to toss him out the huge front window, he wouldn't be able to do a thing about it. He was in good shape and could take care of himself in a tight spot, but wouldn't want to go up against a walking mountain!

Eric reached the table. "Pemberton," he said, nodding slightly and frowning deeply.

"Thanks for coming," Blake said. "Have a seat."

They sat opposite each other, but before either could speak, the waitress appeared with menus.

"We'll order now," Blake said. "I'll have ham on whole wheat and more coffee. Eric?"

"Three roast beefs on rye and milk."

"Hungry, honey?" the waitress asked, smiling a coy smile.

"Not very. I had a big breakfast."

"Oh," she said, and walked away, looking as though she were trying to figure out if Eric had been kidding.

"Okay, Pemberton," Eric said, folding his arms on the table. "I'm here because you said it was about Nickie, and it was important."

"Look," Blake said, "I know you don't like me, but the issue here is Nichelle. I'm asking you to put your feelings toward me aside for now and concentrate on her."

"What about her?"

Blake looked directly at Eric as he spoke. "I'm in love with her, and she loves me. I've asked her to marry me, but she refused. She's scared to death to leave the little world she's woven around herself. You're part of her newfound family, Eric. I need your help."

Eric leaned back in his chair and crossed his arms over his wide chest. The seconds ticked by as the two men stared at each other, and Blake felt a trickle of sweat run down his back. Then, a slow smile tugged at Eric's mouth, and widened into a grin.

"I'll be damned," he said, sitting forward again. "You really love her. I can see it in your eyes, on your face. And you asked her to marry you?"

"Yes."

"You've got a tough road to go, man," he said, shaking his head.

Praise the Lord, Blake thought. Cancel getting tossed out the window. "I know I have a tough road, Eric, but I love Nichelle. There has to be a way to convince her that loving me, marrying me, isn't going to threaten her in any way."

"What has she told you about herself?"

"I know about her father the sleazeball. I just have bits and pieces about her mother. The woman apparently lived in a fantasy world, thinking the louse would come back. From what I gather, she didn't handle money well. Nichelle told me about the bill collectors, the sneaking off in the night."

"Nickie loves you or she wouldn't have told you all that," Eric said, nodding. "But she didn't say why there wasn't any money? She didn't tell you where the money went?"

"No."

"She's protecting her mother's memory, I guess. Nickie told me and Kurt the whole thing, but it was on a night when she fell apart and everything came out. We haven't discussed it in a couple of years. Don't count on getting the rest of the story, Blake. It's too painful for Nickie to relive. And, no, I won't tell you. I respect Nickie's right to keep it to herself."

"I understand where you're coming from, but I'm fighting ghosts, don't you see? Nichelle's past is keeping us from having a future together."

"It would help a helluva lot if you didn't have so much money."

"Come on, Eric." Blake ran his hand over the back of his neck. "Leprechauns, Inc., is doing great financially. Better than great."

"I know, but Nickie is . . . well, sort of pretending it isn't."

"I'm very aware of that. I suggested she buy a house to get a tax break and she flipped out."

"Excuse me, gents," the waitress said. "Lunch is served."

She set their sandwiches and drinks down, and Eric polished off one entire sandwich before he spoke again.

"A house, huh?" he said, picking up another half

of sandwich. "Yeah, that would be nice for her, get her out of that crummy neighborhood."

"It would be a step forward," Blake said. "Later, I'd want to get her a big place where we could raise a family. I want to marry her tomorrow, today. Hell, yesterday, but I realize I'll have to be patient. I have a plan, but I'd need you in on it."

"Pull something sneaky on Nickie? I don't know, Blake. I've decided not to break your face, and I'm convinced you really love Nickie, but . . . what kind of plan?"

"Okay, here it is."

The two men talked for the next hour, during which Eric ate his sandwiches, two pieces of apple pie, and drank a few glasses of milk. Blake managed to eat his own sandwich, but it landed with a thud in his stomach.

"Then we have a deal?" he asked Eric finally.

"I'll give it my best shot, but I'm no actor, and I'm a lousy liar. This could really backfire."

"All we can do is the best we can do. Thanks, Eric."

"I'll see you Saturday if this goes right. When did you sleep last? You look like hell."

"I've had a lot on my mind. A certain little leprechaun is taking up my brain space."

Eric laughed. "Ain't love something'? You're okay, Pemberton. I think you've got what it takes to make Nickie happy. I'll do everything I can to help you, but don't count on me coming up with a miracle."

"Which is probably what I need," Blake said dismally. "Lunch is on me, by the way."

"That's good," Eric said, getting to his feet. "I

have the grand sum of fifty-two cents on me. See ya Saturday. I hope."

"Yeah," Blake said, shaking hands with Eric. "I hope so too."

At six o'clock that evening a nervous Eric was in Nichelle's living room.

"Why?" she asked, frowning up at him.

"Why? Oh, well, because if I look at houses now, it will give me a better idea as to how much more Kurt and I have to save for a down payment. But I need a woman's eye, you know what I mean? I might miss something important. A buddy of mine is a realtor. I got a list of addresses from him and he snuck me a key to the lock boxes. It can't hurt to look and I'll have a better idea what's out there. We'll go Saturday morning about eleven. Call Olivia and tell her you won't be coming to the Pueblo so she won't worry about you. Okay?"

"Oh, I don't know if I want—"

"Great. See you later. I really appreciate this. Mark it on your calendar. It's important, Nickie. 'Bye."

"But . . . well, for Pete's sake," she said to the now-empty room.

At six-thirty Blake called.

"Hi," he said. "How are you?"

"I'm fine. Blake, about last night. I'm sorry I got so upset."

"We're not going to talk about that for now, remember? I love you, you love me. Everything else is on hold. Want to go on a picnic Saturday? It's a little chilly, but we'll dress warm."

"That sounds like fun. What time?"

"How about if I pick you up at eleven?"

"Eleven? Oh, I can't, Blake. I just promised Eric I'd go look at houses with him. He wants to get an idea of costs so he'll know what he and Kurt are facing."

"Oh, I see. Well, what if I tag along? I enjoy looking at houses."

"Eric is going. You know, Eric that you're just so crazy about? The two of you together is a war waiting to happen."

"Not so. Eric and I have had a tense moment or two, but he's basically a nice guy. I won't hassle him. Eric and I are mature adults. We'll get along fine."

"Mmm."

"Then it's all set for Saturday. Listen, I've got a snag in a deal up in San Francisco, and I'm flying up there first thing in the morning. I've got to read a ton of material on it tonight. I really want to see you, but I can't get away."

"I understand. How long will you be gone?"

"I'm not sure. A couple of days, I guess. I'll call you from up there. I'll be back in time to go Saturday morning, that's guaranteed. I love you, Nichelle. Good night."

"Good night, Blake," she said softly, and hung up. She leaned her head onto the back of the sofa and stared at the ceiling. She missed Blake already, she realized. He'd taken her totally off guard with his announcement that he was going out of town. Oh, yes, indeed, the alone would be loneliness without

Blake. But he wasn't gone for good, not yet. He'd be back, and she'd be waiting.

It was foolish, she supposed, to put everything on hold as Blake was insisting they do. Nothing was going to change. Their problems weren't going to disappear. Yes, it was foolish, but it was exactly what she was going to do for now. Just for now, just for a few more stolen hours of happiness.

With a smile on her lips she picked up the telephone and dialed a number.

"Marcella? Hi, it's Nichelle. Want to go out for a pizza?"

Blake pulled the frozen dinner from the microwave and plunked it on the counter, then took a deep swallow from a can of beer.

It was going to be a helluva long week, he thought. It would help immensely if he were really going to San Francisco. But he wasn't, and due to the fact that he, too, was no actor and was a lousy liar, he couldn't run the risk of seeing Nichelle. He had a horrifying image in his mind of walking into her apartment and saying, "Hi. I love you. Saturday morning is a con, a setup to get you to look at houses. How do you like that, sweetheart?"

He shuddered at the thought and dejectedly stuck his fork into his dinner.

"One of these days," he muttered, "this outfit has to come up with unwrinkled peas."

The next morning Blake straightened his tie, put his wallet into his back pocket, and shrugged into his suit jacket. He started toward the bedroom door, then stopped in his tracks.

Cripes! he thought. It was Wednesday! Nichelle was coming to clean his apartment! It had to look as though he'd gone to San Francisco.

He spun around and pulled a suitcase out of the closet. Think! he told himself as he flung it onto the bed. It wasn't what she *would* find in this pig pen that was important, but what she *wouldn't* find; things that should be missing because he'd packed them for his trip. Shaving gear. Check.

He fetched his razor and toothbrush from the bathroom and tossed them into the suitcase. Next came underwear, socks, and ties, a trail of which dotted the floor as he dropped part of his load. He added several shirts, leaving the hangers in plain view on the bed as further evidence. A suit was wadded up and crammed on top of the shirts, then he threw in his brush and comb.

He glanced at his watch, swore, then swore again as he strained to close the bulging suitcase. He'd like to leave a nice note for Nichelle, telling her that he loved her and would miss her, but he didn't dare take the time. She could arrive at any minute, and he couldn't run the risk of seeing her and blurting out the truth.

After a quick glance around the room that now appeared as though it had been trashed by a sadistic burglar, he swung the suitcase off the bed.

Then every muscle in his body tensed.

A key was being inserted in the front door. The door was opening. The door was closed.

"Oh, good Lord," he whispered.

He spun around frantically, then with his heart

thundering in his chest ran into the closet, whacked the suitcase painfully against his knee, and managed to pull the door closed behind him. He mentally recited every swear word he knew.

Nichelle walked into the living room and an indulgent smile formed on her lips.

"Definitely a slob," she said with a laugh as she set her tote bag on the floor. Here she was again, she mused, in Junior Pemberton's messy apartment. But he wasn't Junior, with a different imaginary appearance each Wednesday morning. He was Blake. Blake Tyrone Pemberton, whom she loved so much it nearly made her dizzy when she thought of him. And she wasn't a green-haired alien, not this time. She was Nichelle Clay, whom Blake loved in return.

Almost dreamily she walked to the bedroom, stopping just inside the door to inhale the lingering aroma of Blake's soap and aftershave. She knew he was winging his way to San Francisco, but she could feel his presence here as though he were in the room with her.

"Get to work, Nichelle," she told herself, then grimaced as she saw the trail of clothes on the floor. He'd obviously been in a rush when he'd packed. He'd totally destroyed the place. Well, no matter. As unliberated as it sounded, she would enjoy the hours spent setting Blake's home in order, tending to his needs like a wife. And now she shared the intimate portion of that role as well.

The only thing she couldn't do for Blake was wear the white shawl for him. Yes, she loved him. But the tradition spoke of more, of a lifelong commitment, marriage, a baby, and years together until leaving here for a greater place. The shawl would remain wrapped in tissue and tucked on the closet shelf. The dreams it represented would be quietly tucked away in her heart, unfulfilled.

"Oh, darn," she said with a sigh. No, she wouldn't become gloomy and depressed. She was going to clean and straighten Blake's apartment and have a wonderful time doing it.

She pulled the sheets from the bed, wondering absently how Blake managed to sleep without strangling himself. As she scooped the sheets off the floor, she jerked her head up. She thought she'd seen the closet door move.

Nonsense, she scolded herself, then straightened and turned toward the door. She saw her own reflection in the wide mirror above the dresser.

And saw the eye peering at her from the closet.

The scream Nichelle cut loose with was ear-splitting. She clutched the sheets to her breasts, squeezed her eyes shut, and screamed with every ounce of lung power she possessed.

"Oh, Lord," Blake said, barreling out of the closet. He ran across the room and clamped his hands on her shoulders.

"Aagh!" she continued, volume set on high. "Aagh! Aagh!"

"Nichelle!" he yelled.

"Don't touch me! I have a contagious disease! Go away! Go away!"

He spun her around and shook her slightly. "Nichelle, it's me, Blake. Open your eyes."

She cautiously opened one eye, then the other one flew open. "Blake? What are you doing here? Why were you hiding in the closet? You nearly scared me to death. Why did you do that? You're supposed to be in San Francisco. Why aren't you there?"

She had spoken so fast that Blake had trouble deciphering what she'd said. As her rapid-fire questions separated in his mind and became clear, he knew he was in deep trouble.

"Well?" she asked, narrowing her eyes.

"You certainly have a list of fascinating questions there," he said. He pulled the knot of his tie down several inches. "Real beauts."

"And I'm waiting for answers," she said, tapping her foot.

"I can't converse with someone who's hugging my sheets. It has sexual overtones and is, therefore, distracting. Tell you what. You go start the laundry, then we'll have a nice little chat."

"No." She dropped the sheets in a heap on the floor. "There, I'm no longer hugging your sheets. Why were you hiding in the closet?"

"*You* said I was hiding. *I* never said I was hiding. I could have been looking for something in there, you know."

She glanced at the closet, then looked at him again. "Without turning on the light?" She paused, then her eyes widened. "Blake Pemberton, do you have Miss Six-and-a-half-narrow stashed in there?"

"No! That's a rotten thing to say, Nichelle. I love you, remember? You're the only woman in my life and you know it. Brother, talk about being insulted. You're lucky I'm such a nice guy. Another type would get really ticked off at being accused of such a thing."

"I'm sorry. I really am. I—wait a minute. What am

I apologizing for? You're the one who's acting very suspiciously. You *were* hiding in that closet, Blake."

"Yeah, I know," he said miserably. "Look, I'll call my secretary and tell her I'll be late, then I'll explain everything."

"Why would your secretary be expecting you? You're suposed to be in San Francisco . . . aren't you? Why do I get the feeling I'm not going to like the answers to these questions when I get them?"

"Go make some coffee, okay? I'll call my office."

"Mmm," she said, eyeing him suspiciously as she left the bedroom.

Nichelle was pouring coffee into two mugs when Blake entered the kitchen. He'd taken off his jacket and tie and rolled up the sleeves of his shirt. The unanswered questions in her mind faded into oblivion as her gaze swept over him. But when he picked up the mugs without speaking and went back into the living room, the questions returned, along with a chilling fear. She followed slowly behind him.

They sat together on the sofa, each clutching a mug. Blake was leaning forward, his elbows on his knees, and staring into his steaming coffee. The seconds ticked into minutes. Nichelle's heart thudded against her ribs.

"You're right," he said finally, still looking at his coffee. "I was hiding in the closet. I'd stopped to throw some stuff into a suitcase so it would appear that I'd gone to San Francisco, and you arrived before I could leave."

"You had no intention of going to San Francisco?" she asked quietly, her grip on her mug tightening.

"No. It was an excuse not to see you until Saturday morning."

"An excuse not to see me?" She sat up straighter. "A lie?"

He turned his head to look at her. "Not a lie exactly. It was more like a safety precaution."

"I don't understand. I'm not thrilled with what I'm hearing, but I don't understand."

He set both of their mugs on the coffee table, then shifted to face her, taking one of her hands between his two large ones.

"I couldn't dare see you before Saturday, Nichelle. I'm no more of an actor than Eric is."

"Eric? What does he have to do with this?"

"We met for lunch and . . . do you know how much that guy eats? Never mind. Anyway, at the risk of being tossed through a plate glass window, I asked Eric to meet me. I told him that I loved you, wanted to marry you, and he believed me. He agreed to go along with the plan I'd concocted for Saturday."

"Plan?"

"Eric and Kurt aren't ready to start looking at houses. The idea was for you to go, see what's out there, realize that you're in a position to have a nice home like those we would see. And to realize, Nichelle, that you had nothing to fear by taking that first step forward."

"You and Eric . . . the houses were supposed to . . . I don't believe this." She pulled her hand free and stood up, then walked over to the picture window.

"I knew I'd spill the beans if I saw you, so I invented the trip to San Francisco. I'm sorry, Nichelle. It seemed like a good idea at the time, but I know now that it was wrong. I don't want our relationship to be based on games or tricks. I just thought if I could get you to take one step forward, the rest might come easier for you."

"I see," she said, wrapping her arms around her waist, her back rigid.

"Nichelle, the walls you've built around yourself are so high. I was getting desperate, willing to try anything to get you to believe in me, in the fact that I won't hurt you or allow anything or anyone to hurt you. This plan for Saturday was the pits, though, and I apologize. I'm very, very sorry. I love you, Nichelle. I really do."

Tears misted her eyes as she stared blindly out the window. Her thoughts were racing as she replayed Blake's softly spoken words in her mind.

He'd lied to her! she told herself, blinking away her tears. Even Eric had been in on the lie. Oh, damn, Blake had lied to her.

And . . .

And she had never felt so loved in her entire life.

What Blake had done, he'd done *for* her, not *against* her. He was trying to lead her gently from behind her walls and show her what was beyond them. That she didn't want to go there wasn't important at the moment. What mattered was Blake, and the beautiful depth of his love for her. Dear Lord, how she loved this man.

She heard him get up and cross the room to her. "Nichelle?" he asked, his voice strained. "Will you forgive me? It was a dumb plan and I know you're angry, but I didn't mean to hurt you, I swear it."

She turned to face him. When she saw the worry on his handsome face, fresh tears sprang to her eyes.

"I think," she whispered, "that you are the dearest, sweetest, most wonderful man I have ever known."

"What?" He was obviously confused. "I'm who?"

She smiled. "What should I wear when we go to look at houses?"

"Oh, man." He released a long breath and held out his arms to her. "Come here."

"Can't. I have to do the laundry."

"Come . . . here!"

She laughed as she literally flung herself against him, wrapping her arms around his neck as he held her tightly to him, burying his face in her hair. Then he cupped her head in his hands, tilted it back, and captured her mouth with his.

It was a long and powerful kiss that stole the breath from Nichelle's body and the thoughts from her mind. She was afloat in a passionate, hazy mist as she met Blake's tongue with hers and returned the kiss in total abandon. His hands dropped lower, roaming over her green sweatshirt, her buttocks, then back up to her breasts. She leaned heavily against him, feeling his arousal, all that he was.

"Let me love you," he murmured.

"You have to go to the office," she said breathlessly.

"I'm the boss. I won't fire myself."

"I'm a leprechaun. I have work to do."

"You're *my* leprechaun, and I want you, I need you, I love you. Come to bed with me, Nichelle."

"The sheets are on the floor."

"Then come to the floor with me."

"Yes," she said with what she was sure was the last bit of breath in her body.

"I love you."

"And I love you, Blake Pemberton," she whispered. "I don't want to think further than that right now. Just make love to me. Please."

"The hell with the sheets," he said, and lowered her to the thick, plush carpeting.

Afterward, they lay close, legs entwined. Suddenly Blake chuckled and Nichelle moved her head back to look at him questioningly.

"This is rather bohemian, don't you think?" he said, smiling at her. "I could have at least carried you into the bedroom and made love to you on a bed instead of the living room floor."

"I like it here with the sun streaming in the window."

His smile suddenly vanished. "Will you really look at houses Saturday? A house would be a perfect investment for you, and I'll be with you."

"Yes, I'll look."

"Thank you," he said, and kissed her on the forehead. "You can tell Eric he's off the hook and doesn't have to go. Lord, what a relief. The thought of not seeing you the rest of the week was blowing my mind. Would you like to go out to dinner tonight?"

"Why don't I cook here? I'm very late getting started on your apartment, and I can just stay and have dinner ready when you get home."

"That's an awful lot of work."

"I'll enjoy it. Okay?"

"Sure. I'd be a fool to pass up a home-cooked meal. Well, as much as I hate to move, I really have to get to the office. I'm driving my secretary nuts because she keeps having to change my appointments."

He kissed her, then got to his feet. After scooping up his clothes, he gazed down at her.

"You look beautiful there in the sunlight," he said. "Your skin is rosy from having been with me. You're a vision of loveliness, a woman in love, who has just made love. Incredible."

"You're beautiful too, Blake."

He chuckled as he walked to the bedroom. She stretched leisurely, deciding she'd have no problem whatsoever staying right there in her patch of sunshine. But she had to work, and she sat up reluctantly and reached for her clothes.

After Blake had left, Nichelle started her chores. She laughed and shook her head when she unpacked the suitcase she found in the closet. By late afternoon a roast was in the oven and a peach pie was cooling on the counter. She took a leisurely shower, then pulled on one of Blake's dress shirts. The tail hung almost to her knees. As she was setting the table in the dining room, the telephone rang.

"Hello?" she said cheerfully.

"Mr. Pemberton, please."

"I'm sorry he isn't home yet. May I take a message?"

"I called his office but he'd already left. He must be en route. This is Betty Jefferson from the Willow Tree Country Club. I'm in charge of reservations for the dinner-dance Saturday night. Mrs. Easterman told me that Mr. Pemberton said he was definitely planning on attending, yet I have no record of his reservation. Would you ask Mr. Pemberton to call me here at the club as soon as he gets in?"

Nichelle instantly recalled the conversation with the Eastermans in the restaurant. "Oh, Blake just said he was going to the dance to . . . well, I'll let him tell you. I'll give him your message."

"Thank you. I appreciate it. This is a gala event and I'm sure he won't want to miss it. Mr. Pemberton is one of our most active members. Thanks again. Good-bye."

"Good-bye," Nichelle said, and replaced the receiver. She stood staring at the telephone as the woman's words hammered against her mind. Blake was one of the most active members of the country club? She'd gotten the impression that night in the restaurant that he wasn't at all interested in the whole thing.

At the sound of a key being inserted in the door she spun around, and a moment later Blake entered the apartment.

"Oh, yes, you are nice to come home to," he said, his eyes glowing as he took in her slender form clad in his shirt. He crossed the room, pulled her into his arms, and kissed her. "You smell good, taste good, look good. I thought this day would never end so I could get home to you. I'll change out of this suit as soon as I kiss you six more times."

"Wait," she said. "You had a phone call."

"Oh?"

"You're supposed to call Betty Jefferson at the Willow Tree Country Club regarding your reservations for Saturday night. Apparently, Mrs. Easterman told her you were planning on going."

"Oh." He stepped back and shrugged out of his suit coat. He tugged off his tie, then pulled his shirt free of his pants.

"Betty Jefferson said you're one of their most active members," Nichelle continued, watching his face carefully.

"Well, yeah, I suppose I am. I keep my boat there, play tennis, swim. I've served on several fund-raising committees for college scholarships for low-income kids. I've gone to a lot of the social events the club puts on. There are all ages at the club, and activities to suit everyone."

"I didn't realize you enjoyed it that much," she said quietly. "That wasn't the impression I got when you spoke to the Eastermans."

"I was just trying to get them to mosey on down the trail. But I thoroughly enjoy the club. You will too."

"Me?"

"Yes, Nichelle, you," he said, looking directly at her. "I'd like you to attend that dinner-dance with me Saturday night. I want you to go with me, meet my friends, just like I did when I went with you to the Pueblo. This is important to me, Nichelle. I want you at that dance." He turned and started toward the bedroom. "I'll change my clothes now."

No! Nichelle screamed silently. It was bad enough that she'd fantasized all day, pretending she belonged in Blake's Bel Air apartment. But to cross farther over the line? Go to a country club, mingle with the wealthy, even famous people there. She couldn't, she just couldn't. Blake had to understand that she couldn't go. Oh, please, she begged, make him understand!

Nine

In the bedroom Blake changed into jeans and a burgundy-colored shirt, then sat down on the bed. He knew he was pushing Nichelle again, but he'd thought about it the entire time he'd been driving home. Just as he was leaving the office, his secretary had called after him that Betty Jefferson was on the phone. He told his secretary to tell Betty he'd already left. He'd wanted to get home to Nichelle with no more delays, and could call Betty from the apartment.

But during the drive in the rush-hour traffic, he'd sorted things through in his mind. The plan for having Nichelle look at houses Saturday had fallen apart due to the fact that it was just that—a plan, a scheme. Yes, she was going to go look at houses, but he'd be kidding himself if he thought she was going to give any serious consideration to buying one.

No, he mused, she was going because he'd confessed his dastardly deed, and had literally begged her to forgive him for deceiving her. It was a peacemaking gesture on her part, a way of showing him she wasn't angry for what he'd done. He might as well face the fact that he'd made no real progress at chipping away at Nichelle's walls. He was back to square one.

He got up and paced back and forth, then sank back onto the neatly made bed again.

What he'd told Nichelle was true, he thought. He *did* enjoy the events at the club, and he *was* a very active member. He had good friends there, some even dating back to his childhood. Sure, there were a few snobs among the membership, but he avoided them, just like he'd ignored the few people who'd thrown hostile glances at him at the Pueblo.

He worked hard at the club, too, serving on committees that would benefit others. He was proud of the accomplishments achieved by those committees, and he benefited from the workouts on the courts, in the gym, and in the pool. The quiet time spent out on his boat cleared his mind, and gave him a chance to regroup.

There was nothing at Willow Tree Country Club to frighten Nichelle Clay.

Yes, he thought, it was important to him that Nichelle come to that dance Saturday night. Oh, not to the dance, per se, but he needed her to cross over that damn invisible line of hers and trust him. Trust him to show her a slice of his life, a place and people that held special meaning for him.

That was the bottom line. Nichelle had to be willing to meet him halfway, to compromise, if they were to have any chance of making it together. And in order to meet him halfway, she'd have to come out from behind her walls. He had to know. He had to know if she really had any intention of doing that.

He'd worked hard for what he had, and, unlike Nichelle, enjoyed the rewards of that labor. Sure, he liked the Pueblo and its earthy honesty, but he also got satisfaction from skimming across the water in an expensive boat, feeling the wind and spray on his face, and knowing he'd earned every minute of that pleasure.

Nichelle had earned the right to have what she wanted too, Blake reasoned. Leprechauns, Inc., was a highly successful enterprise. But the question remained: what *did* she want? Did she intend to stay in her safe little world? Did she assume Blake would be willing to join her there, sharing the limited space with the ghosts of her past? No, it wouldn't work. She had to trust him, love him enough to place her hand in his and step forward.

"Blake," she called. "Are you coming? Dinner is on the table."

"I'm putting on my shoes," he answered. "I'll be right there." Complete with a knot in his gut, he thought dryly. A helluva lot was riding on this evening.

He walked slowly from the bedroom to the dining room, forcing a smile onto his face. He watched Nichelle place a juicy roast on the table. She looked so sexy wearing his shirt, and the heat of desire rocketed through him. He wanted to forget Willow Tree Country Club and all it represented. Forget the Pueblo and the statement it made. Forget the damn line drawn across the city. He just wanted Nichelle in his arms, his. But he couldn't do that, and he knew it.

"Looks great," he said. "Need some help?"

"No," she said, pouring the wine into glasses. "Just sit and enjoy. Everything is ready. I hope you don't mind my borrowing your shirt." She sat down opposite him and fiddled with her napkin, avoiding looking at him. "I wanted to put on something fresh after my shower. I unpacked that suitcase, by the way. Good thing you weren't really planning on wearing those things. They were a wrinkled mess. Then I—"

"Nichelle."

"I did the laundry, of course," she rushed on, serving meat to both of them. "Help yourself to the vegetables. I'm sure you're hungry after—"

"Nichelle, stop it."

"What?" she asked, slowly meeting his gaze.

"Talking a blue streak isn't going to make it go away."

"I'm just chatting."

"No, you're babbling with the hope there won't be room or time to discuss the country club dance."

"I'm doing no such thing." She paused. "Yes, I am."

He scooped vegetables onto his plate, picked up his fork, put it down again, and reached for her hand.

"Listen to me," he said gently. "We're not just talking about a dance here. Do you realize that?"

"Yes, I do," she said, her voice trembling. "It's more than a dance, it's a way of life. It represents a certain class of people, standards, values."

"None of which are threatening. Yes, we play, if you want to use that word, at the country club and we have expensive toys. But we also work. The committee I'm on at the moment is coordinating its efforts with the free food bank. It's not just the idle rich lounging around the pool deciding where to jet off to next for a high old time. It's people, Nichelle. Some good, some bad, just like in the Pueblo."

"Just like—" She pulled her hand free. "How can you even compare the two groups?"

"Because they're not that different," he said, his voice starting to rise. "Dammit, Nichelle, you're standing in judgment of the people at the country club and you don't even know them."

"Oh, I know them," she said bitterly. "I've known them all of my life. I understand how they think, what their values are. My father was one of them, is still one of them."

"He has nothing to do with us, don't you see? You've never even met the man, yet he's standing between us, keeping us apart. Let the past go, Nichelle. Put it away. Look to the future, *our* future."

"Just forget it all happened?" she asked, getting to her feet. "Forget that my mother died by inches over the years because of that man?"

"It's over!"

"For my mother, yes. But I don't intend to forget the lessons I learned from what I went through with her. She was a clerk in a clothing store, an expensive clothing store. My father came in to buy some shirts and she waited on him. That night at closing, he was outside waiting for her. He told her he hadn't been able to get her off his mind."

"And?" Blake asked, his gaze riveted to her face.

"He took her to dinner, then drove her home in his fancy car. She was living in a dingy little apartment all alone. He left her at the door, but the next day he sent her flowers, and after work he was waiting for her again. Every day for two weeks he sent her flowers, took her to dinner at plush restaurants, then left her at her door with nothing more than a kiss good night. Then—" Nichelle stopped speaking and took a deep breath.

"Then?" Blake prodded.

"He said that he loved her. She loved him so much by then herself, and his declaration of love was a dream come true. That night she invited him into her apartment and her bed. The pattern was established. He'd pick her up after work, take her to dinner, then they'd go to her apartment and make love. He never stayed the whole night, but she didn't mind because he'd always be waiting for her the next night."

"And then she got pregnant."

"Yes. She was thrilled, so happy. She could hardly wait to tell him. They'd get married, of course. But it didn't work out that way."

"What happened?"

Tears sprang to Nichelle's eyes. "He was furious, called my mother an irresponsible fool. He threw a handful of money on the table and told her to get an abortion. He screamed at her, told her that she wouldn't get another cent from him. He'd only been filling his time with her while his fiancée was in Europe shopping for her trousseau. He—he sneered at my mother, Blake, told her she wasn't good enough to be his wife. He said she'd better learn where her place was, where she belonged, and stay there."

"Damn," Blake said, his hands curling into tight fists. "Damn him."

"But my mother never gave up," Nichelle continued, a hollowness to her voice as she stared into space. "She told herself he'd come for her, for us. When I was ten she read in the paper that he'd gotten a divorce. She used the rent money to buy an expensive outfit, then went to his office to see him. He ordered her out, told her to never come near him again."

"My God," Blake whispered, feeling his fury build.

"She was obsessed with him. She followed him wherever he went. She spent every cent she could get her hands on to buy clothes to impress him. She'd eat at the same restaurants as he did, joined the health club he belonged to. It was just a matter of time, she'd tell me, before he quit denying his love for her. He'd see how beautiful she was, know she *was* good enough for him, and he'd come for us. But it was the bill collectors who came, and we'd have to run away in the night."

Blake stood up. "Nichelle, I'm so sorry."

"Then," she went on as though she weren't aware that he had spoken, "it was announced in the paper that he'd married a wealthy socialite. My mother had a heart attack. She gave up then, on him, on life. Within months she was totally bedridden, and then"—tears spilled onto her cheeks—"she died."

"Nichelle . . ."

"No." She raised her hand. "You've got to listen, understand. There *is* a line, Blake. There is! I'm stepping over it by being here with you as your lover instead of just your cleaning lady. This is a mistake, and I won't go further. I won't. I can't. The price is too high, the pain too great. I've got to stay where I belong!"

"No!" He grabbed her by the shoulders. "You're not your mother, and I'm not your father. You're mixing us all up together, and that's not fair. I love you, Nichelle, and I want you to be my wife. I don't care if you have fifty dollars or fifty thousand. It doesn't matter."

"Yes, it does," she said shrilly.

"Only to you. Okay, fine. I'll respect that. But, dammit, you have Leprechauns, Inc. I'd give you everything I have, but it isn't even necessary. You've earned it yourself. You can have what you want, go where you please. There's no line drawn for you, Nichelle."

"Yes, there is, and there's nothing beyond that line I want!"

He went very still. Slowly he dropped his hands from her shoulders and took a step backward. Pain flickered across his face, then settled in his gray eyes.

"*I'm* across that line," he said, his voice low. "Me, and my love, and the life we could share together."

"No," she sobbed, shaking her head. "I can't, I can't." She pushed past him and ran from the room.

"*Damn!*" Blake swore as he stared at the ceiling. "Nichelle, please, please, don't do this to us. I love you. I need you." He walked slowly into the living room, acutely aware of the knot in his stomach and the lump in his throat.

Nichelle came out of the bedroom dressed in her jeans and sweatshirt. They stopped, a room apart, but to Nichelle it was a world apart, an expanse greater than she had the courage or strength to cross. Their eyes met, hers misted by tears, his also unusually bright.

"Good-bye, Blake," she whispered.

"No, don't say that," he said, his voice husky. "We can work it all out, Nichelle, if we do it together. We'll fight your ghosts and win. I'll be right there with you every minute. I love you so much. Nichelle, please."

She stumbled forward, tears blurring her vision as she reached for her tote bag. She choked on a sob, and her aching heart hammered against her ribs. On trembling legs she ran into the foyer and out the front door.

"Nichelle!" he yelled. "No!"

He started after her, then stopped, fury and pain twisting within him. He picked up a figurine from an end table and hurled it across the room. The china flew in all directions as it smashed against the wall. And then silence. A chilling silence broken only by Blake's labored breathing.

"Oh, God," he said suddenly. It was getting dark and Nichelle was alone on the bus. Weirdos, maniacs were on those buses.

He ran into the bedroom for his wallet and keys, then hurried from the apartment. The delicious dinner was still sitting on the table, totally forgotten.

Over an hour later Blake pushed himself away from the tree he'd been leaning against across the street from Nichelle's apartment building. His fists clenched as he watched her walk slowly down the sidewalk. When she reached the doors to the building she stopped, seemed to draw a deep breath, then squared her shoulders and went inside.

His entire body ached from the tight restraint he was forcing upon himself to keep from running after her. He wanted to haul her into his arms, tell her they'd live totally in her world, complete with the ghosts and fears. But he couldn't, he knew it, and the realization brought a cold, lonely wave of depression washing over him.

"I've lost my leprechaun," he said quietly. "Goodbye, Nichelle."

Nichelle walked wearily down the hall toward her apartment. She was exhausted, and every step she took threatened to draw the last ounce of energy from her body. During the long bus ride home she'd replayed over and over in her mind the final scene in Blake's apartment. Fresh tears continually filled her eyes as she saw the pain on Blake's face time and again. She had hurt, and lost, the only man she had ever loved, and her heart felt as though it were splintering into a million pieces.

At least Eric and Kurt were both at work, she thought. If either of them had been there to smile or say one sweet word to her, she'd dissolve in a puddle of tears.

"Hey, Nickie. How's the prettiest leprechaun on the face of the earth?"

That did it. She looked up, saw Eric smiling at her from the door of his apartment, and burst into tears.

"Uh-oh," he said, hurrying toward her. "There's trouble in paradise."

"Why aren't you bouncing people around at the club?" she asked, sniffling. She burrowed in her tote bag for her key.

"They're remodeling the crummy joint. What's wrong?"

"Nothing."

"I can see that," he said, following her into her apartment. "Since I have nothing to do, explain the nothing that has you so shook up." He closed the door and led her by the hand to the sofa. "Sit." She sat. "Well?"

"I don't want to talk about it," she said, pulling a tissue from her tote bag. "It's over, finished. He said . . . then I said . . . and I've never been so miserable in my entire life," she wailed as fresh tears spilled onto her cheeks.

"Nickie, am I back to having to break Pemberton's face?"

"No! Don't you touch him. I love him with every breath in my body. He's the dearest, warmest, most wonderful man I've ever known."

"Sure, he is," Eric said, nodding. "That's why you're so happy. I'm definitely going to break his face."

"You go near him and I'll never again lie to your aunt Myrtle Ann, and tell her that you and I are engaged, and that we plan to adopt Kurt."

"You're not being nice, Nickie."

"Then quit threatening the man I love."

"Fine, fine. Tell me the nothing he did to you to make you cry."

"He—he wanted me to go to a dance."

"Yeah, well, that's perverted, all right," Eric said, obviously confused. "The man is sick." He dropped into a chair and frowned. "That's it?"

"Then he said . . . then I said . . . ohhh," she moaned, and buried her face in her hands.

"Nickie," Eric yelled, "spit it out. Every word. From the top. Now!"

And she did. With tears streaming down her face she told Eric everything that had happened. She cried her way through her tale, shredded a half-dozen tissues, then finally leaned her head back and closed her eyes. Eric said nothing, and when the silence had stretched into nerve-racking minutes, she opened one eye and peered at him. He had a blank expression on his face.

"I've finished," she said, opening both eyes and lifting her head. "Aren't you going to say anything?"

"I was just thinking," he said quietly.

"About what I told you?"

"About how you tolerate all of us."

"What? What do you mean?"

"Well, see, I understand where you're coming from. You know, the way you have to stay where you belong, not try to be something you're not, and sure as hell not go to a fancy dance or marry an uptown guy."

"Thank you, Eric. I knew I could count on you."

"Thing is, how can you stomach the rest of us? Take me and Kurt, for example. We're going to buy a house, get out of this scummy neighborhood. That takes gall. Then there's Marcella. She's working for you while she's going to UCLA. Imagine the nerve of her wanting to be a teacher, to have a better life than she had in the barrio. Pushy broad. Who does she think she is to go around exhausted all the time just so she can have a higher standard of living?"

"But—"

"And Olivia. Olivia, who cried tears of joy because Kurt and I painted her home and made it special. She has the only house on that grungy block that's fresh and clean, and shows some pride of owner-

hip. How dare we, all of us, not stay where we
elong and leave things as they are?"

"Oh, but, Eric—"

"You're the only one who has her head on straight,
Iickie. You're going to live right here alone, forever,
ehashing every mistake your mother made to re-
nind you that the past is more important than the
uture. No, sir, we won't find you screwing around
vith hopes and dreams for tomorrow. Hell, you're
oo sensible for that. I'm sure glad you dusted
'emberton off before you messed up and let your
ove rule your emotions."

"I . . ."

"You're an amazing woman," Eric said, getting to
is feet. "Really amazing. And generous, too, to put
p with the rest of us poor slobs, who forget yester-
ay, accept today, and work and dream for a better
omorrow. Well, it was nice chatting with you. I have
go match up the colored stripes on my sweat
ocks. See ya."

"But . . . but . . ." she stammered as the door
losed behind Eric. She blinked, then blinked again.
othing he had said made any sense.

Or did it?

She stood up and began pacing. Memories of her
nother flooded her mind, along with the pain, the
mbarrassment she had felt at her mother's blind
evotion to a man who obviously had used her, who
ad never loved her.

But somehow the pain was less sharp than it had
een before, the image of her mother less clear.
nstead, Nichelle was more aware of the warmth and
y she had felt with Blake. His face was predomi-
ant in her mind. What had he said? That there
as no line drawn for her?

And Eric. What had he meant when he said she'd remain here alone, forever, rehashing every mistake her mother had made to remind her that the past was more important than the future? Was that what she was doing? How awful!

She continued pacing, continued thinking, until slowly the pieces began to fall into place. Blake was right. And so was Eric. Everything was clear now, as though a burst of sunshine had suddenly revealed a path to free her from a dark, tangled maze, to give her the gifts of hopes and dreams, tomorrows and love. And Blake.

"If it's not too late," she whispered. "Oh, Blake I'm so sorry. I was such a frightened, foolish child."

She ran to the door, flung it open, and collided with the hard wall of Eric's body. She threw her arms around his neck.

"Thank you, thank you, thank you," she said. "I love you, Eric."

"And I love you, Nickie. You're going to like it in the world of hopes and dreams, you'll see."

"I know I will. I just pray it's not too late to make it up to Blake."

"You're a leprechaun, remember? Work some magic. In the meantime, come help me match sweat socks."

Late the next afternoon Nichelle took a deep, steadying breath, then dialed the number she'd memorized.

"Willow Tree Country Club," a woman said.

"Hello, darling," Nichelle said dramatically. That was a bit much, she decided. Not all rich people talked like phony baloneys. "May I speak to Betty Jefferson, please?"

"This is Betty."

"Oh, well, this is Miss Clay, daughter of Jack and Esther, and I have a teensy little problem."

"How may I help you, Miss Clay?"

"You see, I planned to attend the dance with Blake—Junior Pemberton, Saturday night, but I wasn't sure if I'd be in town. Now Blake—Junior is away, and I don't know if he made a reservation for us. Get it? I mean, do you comprehend my dilemma?"

"Certainly. Let me check the list."

Nichelle pressed a trembling hand to her forehead and waited.

"Miss Clay?"

"What?" she said, jumping in her chair. She cleared her throat. "Yeees?"

"Blake Pemberton, Jr., made a reservation only for himself. Shall I confirm yours for both dinner and dancing?"

"Just the dance," Nichelle said. She'd be so nervous she'd never choke down a bite of food. "I'm on a very tight schedule."

"Fine. I've taken care of it. We'll look forward to seeing you Saturday night. The dancing will begin at ten."

"Thank you ever so very much and . . . whatever. 'Bye." She hung up quickly, then sprawled in her chair and released a rush of air. "Step one is fait accompli. Oh, Lord, I'm not going to survive this."

"Don't you agree, Blake?" Blake Pemberton, Sr., asked.

"Yes, certainly," Blake said, staring into his champagne glass.

"Do you also agree that the entire state of California is going to fall into the ocean at noon tomorrow?"

"Hmmm? Oh, yeah, sure thing, Dad."

Blake, Sr., chuckled. "Son, your body showed up at this shindig, but your mind didn't tag along. You hardly touched your dinner, the band is on the third song and you haven't danced, and you look like you've lost your best friend."

"Sorry," Blake said, and drained the glass.

"She must be quite a woman."

Blake looked blankly at his father. "Who?"

"The one who has you tied up in knots and resembling a pouting basset hound. Your mother is dancing with Judge Munroe. Is there anything you want to discuss before she gets back? Who is the woman?"

"She's a leprechaun," Blake said, snatching another glass of champagne from the tray of a passing waiter.

"Oh? How much of that stuff have you had to drink? Where did you meet her?"

"She beamed down into my bedroom when she was a green-haired alien."

"I'm putting you in a taxi. You're drunk as a skunk, my boy. You don't look drunk, but—Say now, if you want to take your mind off of your problems, look at what just came into the ballroom. That is a lovely, lovely woman. I've never seen her before."

"Not interested," Blake said gruffly.

"You're not drunk, you're dead. Her dress is quite nice. Sort of sea green and draped in a classic style. But I think she looks . . . oh, angelic, I'd say, because of that white shawl. It's exquisite."

Blake snapped his head up and his eyes widened as he stared across the room. His heart thundered in his chest and he swallowed heavily.

"My God," he whispered, "it's Nichelle. And—and she's wearing the white shawl."

"It's who?" his father asked.

"My leprechaun. Here." Blake shoved the glass at him.

"Drunk as a skunk," Blake, Sr., said, shaking his head as Blake strode away. "Shame on him."

Oh, what an asinine plan this was, Nichelle thought frantically. It was so crowded in here, she'd never find Blake. And if she did find him, what if he refused to speak to her? And what if someone discovered she'd impersonated Jack and Esther's darling daughter and tossed her out? Oh, she wanted to go home.

And then she saw him.

Blake Tyrone Pemberton, Jr., dressed in a perfectly cut tuxedo that made him look like one of the waiters in that fancy restaurant, was working his way through the crowd toward her.

He was beautiful. He was Blake. She loved him so very much, and her heartbeat was echoing in her ears.

He stopped about three feet away from her. His gaze swept over her face, the shawl, then returned to her face, as though he were searching for answers.

"Nichelle?" he said, his eyes locked with hers. "You're here? You're wearing the white shawl? Nichelle?"

There was so much to say to him, she realized. She had to beg his forgiveness for being so foolish, for hurting him. She wanted to declare her love over and over, and talk of the future, their tomorrows.

But not here in this crowded room. And so, for now, she'd answer his questions as clearly and as simply as possible.

"Yes, I'm here. And, yes, I'm wearing the white shawl just for you, forever."

Blake squeezed his eyes tightly closed as he gathered his emotions. He was smiling when he opened them again and extended his hand to her.

"May I have this dance, future Mrs. Pemberton, Jr.?"

"It will be my pleasure, Mr. Pemberton," she said, placing her hand in his.

He drew her close. "Welcome to my world."

"*Our* world," she said, smiling through her tears. "I love you so much, Blake."

"And I love you. The hell with stuffy protocol," he muttered, then took possession of her mouth in a powerful kiss.

Across the room Blake Pemberton, Sr., laughed in delight and lifted his glass in a toast.

"Here's to leprechauns," he said, beaming. "I think we're about to have one in the family!"

THE EDITOR'S CORNER

Thanks for all your wonderful cards and letters telling us how glad you are that we've added two LOVESWEPTS to our monthly publishing list. Obviously, it's quite a lot of additional work, and, so, we are especially glad to welcome Kate Hartson as our new senior editor. Kate has been in publishing for more than seven years and has edited many different kinds of works, but in the last few years she has devoted a great deal of her time to romance fiction and has edited almost one hundred love stories. Kate is as fine a person as she is an editor, and we are delighted to have her on our team.

You have six delicious treats to anticipate next month from Peggy Webb, Sandra Brown, Joan Elliott Pickart, Kay Hooper, Charlotte Hughes, and Iris Johansen. I probably don't need to say more than those six names to make you eager to get at the books—but I had so much fun working on them that it would be virtually impossible for me to restrain myself from sharing my enthusiasm with you.

Peggy Webb presents a heartrending love story in **PRIVATE LIVES,** LOVESWEPT #216. John Riley is a man whose brilliant singing career has left him somewhat burned out; Sam Jones is an enchanting woman who blunders into his rural retreat and brings more sunshine and fresh tickling breezes into his life than he could get in the great outdoors. This moving romance is a bit of a departure into more serious emotional writing for Peggy, though she doesn't leave her characteristic humor behind. Her lovers are wonderful, and we think their healing power on each other will leave you feeling marvelous long after you've finished reading about their **PRIVATE LIVES.**

FANTA C, Sandra Brown's LOVESWEPT #217, is a sheer delight. On the surface heroine Elizabeth Burke seems to be a bit straitlaced, but her occupation—and her daydreams—reveal her to be a sensual and romantic lady. She owns and operates a boutique in a large hotel called Fantasy, where she sells such items as silk lingerie and seductive perfumes. It is in her rich and powerful fantasy life that she expresses her real self . . . until neighbor Thad Randolph comes to her rescue, dares to fulfill her secret dreams, and turns fantasy into reality. A keeper, if there ever was one!

LUCKY PENNY by Joan Elliott Pickart is LOVESWEPT #218 and another real winner from this talented and prolific author. Penelope Chapman is a complicated woman with a wealth of passion and sweet sympathy beneath her successful exterior. Cabe Malone is a man who secretly yearns for a woman to cherish and build a life with. They meet when Cabe finds her weeping in the house he is building . . . and his very protective instinct is aroused. Soon, though, Penny must flee, and Cabe sets off in hot pursuit. A breathlessly exciting chase ensues, and you'll cheer when these two lovable people capture each other.

News Flash! Kay Hooper is being held hostage by a band of

(continued)

dangerous, sexy men, and they aren't going to let her go until she's finished telling the love story of each and every one of them. And aren't we lucky? Fasten your seatbelts, because with **RAFFERTY'S WIFE,** LOVESWEPT #219, Kay is going to sweep you away on another glorious caper. This time that sneaky Hagen has Rafferty Lewis and Sarah Cavell in his clutches. He's assigned them the roles of husband and wife on an undercover assignment that takes them to an island paradise in the midst of revolution. But Rafferty and Sarah are falling deeply, hopelessly in love, and their madness for each other is almost as desperate as the job they have to do. Watch out for Sereno . . . and don't think that just because Raven and Josh are on their honeymoon they are going to be out of the romantic action. It's only fair to tell you that Kay has created a marvelous series for you. Look next for **ZACH's LAW,** then **THE FALL OF LUCAS KENDRICK,** then . . . well, more on this from me next month!

Exciting, evocative, and *really original* aptly describe, LOVESWEPT #220, **STRAIGHT SHOOTIN' LADY** by Charlotte Hughes. When Maribeth Bradford comes to the bank in her small town to interview with its handsome new president for a job, she walks into a robbery in progress. Suddenly, she finds herself bound back-to-back with devastatingly attractive Edward Spears and locked with him in a dark closet. . . . And that's just the beginning of a great love story between a devoted small-town gal and a city slicker with a lot of adjustments to make. We think you're going to be utterly charmed by this wonderful romance.

THE SPELLBINDER, LOVESWEPT #221, by Iris Johansen delivers precisely what the title promises—a true spellbinder of a love story. Brody Devlin can hypnotize an audience as easily as he can overwhelm a woman with his virile good looks. Sacha Lorion is a waif with wild gypsy beauty who has a claim on Brody. Her past is dark, mysterious, dangerous . . . and when her life is threatened, Brody vows to protect her. Both of them swiftly learn that they must belong to one another body and soul . . . 'til death do them part. This is a magnificent story full of force and fire.

Enjoy!

Sincerely,

Carolyn Nichols

Carolyn Nichols
Editor

LOVESWEPT
Bantam Books, Inc.
666 Fifth Avenue
New York, NY 10103